SOMETHING WATCHING

Other books by Hugh Scott

Freddie and the Enormouse
The Summertime Santa

For older readers

The Camera Obscura
The Haunted Sand
The Plant that Ate the World
The Shaman's Stone
Why Weeps the Brogan?

SOMETHING WATCHING

HUGH SCOTT

WALKER BOOKS
LONDON

First published 1990 by Walker Books Ltd
87 Vauxhall Walk, London SE11 5HJ

© 1990 Hugh Scott

First printed 1990
Printed and bound in Great Britain by
Billings & Sons Ltd, Worcester

Typeset by 🅰 Tek Art Ltd
Addiscombe, Croydon, Surrey

British Library Cataloguing in Publication Data
Scott, Hugh
Something watching.
I. Title
823'.914 [F]
ISBN 0-7445-1549-1

For the original Blobby
Fiona Brodie

ONE

Father was just a little bit drunk.

"Daddy," said Alice suspiciously. Her toe touched the cork of a champagne bottle as she stepped towards him. In the kitchen Mother was singing. "All right," said Alice in her best policeman's voice, "what's going on? Mum," she called, "what's happening and where's my share of the booze and why wasn't I told about this?"

Mother came through clutching a tray with the Sunday teapot steaming on it, and Grandma's Royal Doulton plates, one with sandwiches, the other bulging with meringues.

Father divided the last of the champagne, half filling a clean glass for Alice.

"Still snowing?" he asked innocently.

Since snowflakes were slipping down the window thickly enough to blot out the bungalows across the road, Father's question deserved not to be answered.

Alice tapped her foot and tightened her lips. She knew her cheeks stuck out when she did this, but she also knew that Father couldn't resist. His finger and thumb tugged warmly at her face.

"Shall we tell her?" he asked Mother. He handed Alice the half glass of champagne.

"Tell her before I burst!" cried Mother.

"Well," said Father. He fumbled inside the jacket of his suit. Alice tightened her cheeks even more, pulling her brows down.

An envelope jutted up from between her father's lean fingers. A large blue envelope, full of importance. The address contained Dad's name, Richard A.L. Mason Esq.

"Since Christmas is only weeks away," he said lovingly, "and you didn't have much of a thirteenth birthday due to the oven burning your birthday cake, and—"

"Daddy!" growled Alice.

"I bought you a castle."

Snowflakes rushed against the window in astonishment, white-eyed, darkening the room. Behind Father the gas fire brightened.

Alice dragged her woolly hat down off her hair. Her thoughts bumped about in confusion, not knowing if Daddy had said something wonderful or something terrible; not knowing if he meant it, or —

"It's a joke," whispered Alice.

Father beamed.

"Does nobody want this tea?" asked Mother.

"You mean a toy castle. I'm too old for toys."

"Real castle," grinned Father, "and here's to it!" He held his glass towards Alice.

She tasted her champagne, and for a moment her scattered thoughts paid attention to the dry sweet fizz in her mouth. Then she threw her hat into an armchair, unwrapped herself from her thick soft coat, and began her questions. Where? When are we moving? How can we afford it? How big is it?

"Whoa!" said Dad.

"But you always consult me!" cried Alice.

"About holidays! Or wallpaper!" Alice scowled at her mother. "That's why the house has been so tidy these last few weeks. You've had people in to look round. Is this house sold?"

"It was a surprise," said Mother. "Let's sit down and have our tea and sandwiches. I'll make a proper meal later."

"Don't be hurt," said Daddy. "We didn't tell you because we weren't sure, and didn't want to build up your hopes. And no, the castle wasn't horribly expensive. There's no demand for castles. The money we get for this house will pay for it, and some left over. The expense will be keeping the place warm and rebuilding and redecorating, and no doubt ten thousand other things we haven't thought about! No, it hasn't got a moat, but there are trees all round, yes and rocks and sea —"

"It's on the coast!" said Mother excitedly. "Oh, Dick, have we done the right thing?" She answered herself immediately. "Of course we have. But the work will be tremendous. You'll need to help, Alice."

Alice's thoughts turmoiled like mice while Mother chattered and Father read for the third time the lawyer's letter in the blue envelope, which declared firmly that the castle and its environs from the high-tide mark on the north beach to the ancient marches by the stream, the orchard, courtyard, stables, outbuildings etc. etc. etc., were indeed the property of Richard Allander Lane Mason presently residing at . . .

The tower of sandwiches shrank to its foundations. The meringues disappeared leaving Grand-

9

ma's plate with crumbs on its painted roses.

Hours melted into the heat of their talk.

The talk clattered among dishes as the table was set – eventually.

Dinner passed their tongues untasted.

Alice was warm and full up, and excited. She only realized she was sleepy when Mother said, "Bed." She went willingly, up inside the little chalet bungalow, step by step on the red carpet. She hadn't noticed the carpet's colour before.

She stood in her room, just looking. She had outgrown the ducks on the wallpaper – paper she had chosen. The white paint of the window-sill was scored and stained. Her books, scattered on the floor lay half hidden under clothes and album covers, magazines, a postcard . . .

Mother had kept the secret of the house being for sale by not tidying Alice's room. People must have just put their heads round the door, because there was hardly space to walk.

Alice was suddenly embarrassed. She began to tidy, making a laundry pile. Books became a little library on her chest of drawers. Spilled coins went into the ashtray of African silver, among her earrings.

By tidying, she was somehow saying goodbye to her room.

She went to the bathroom and cried as she cleaned her teeth. She wasn't really sad, but she knew that part of her life was being left behind.

And deep inside herself, deeper inside than you can possibly imagine – she was frightened.

TWO

The hall smelt of newspaper. Alice leaned against the front door, shutting out the snow-filled wind.

She couldn't move for boxes. Cardboard boxes stacked emptily inside each other. Open boxes half packed with crushed newspaper with cup handles peeping out. Mother really had started packing too early, thought Alice, though – she supposed – there was a great deal to do.

She slung her schoolbag up the staircase. She hauled off her wellingtons, then walked carefully, her brown-stockinged ankles avoiding cardboard corners.

"Mum!"

"In here, darling."

Mother was kneeling by the gas fire in the lounge, pulling from a flat dusty box, a coat, wrapped in tissue paper.

"Where did you get that!" cried Alice.

"It was Grandma Parker's, I suppose," said Mother. "Though I don't remember her ever wearing it. It was in the loft. There are things up there I don't even recognize, they've been stored so long. It's beautiful!" She stood up till the coat hung its full heavy length, the tissue paper dropping away.

"It's an animal!" said Alice.

"Leopard, I think," said Mother.

"It's cruel!"

"Oh, but isn't it magnificent!"

Alice, staring at the crisp fur patterned like paw prints on sand, nodded.

She became very still.

Mother chattered, turning the coat this way and that, shaking it, draping it over her arm to peer at the lining – and Alice stood inside her own head, looking out.

It was very odd. She suddenly felt like a visitor in her own body; as if she could step away, and leave herself standing. She sensed the soles of her stockings pressed between her feet and the carpet, and her teeth neatly clenched in the darkness of her mouth.

Her eyes moved, following the dropping folds as Mother turned the coat. A paper label danced on string attached inside the collar. Mother caught it and crinkled her eyes.

"*This coat*," she read, "*must be*. . . It looks like, *burned*. Surely it's *cleaned?*"

"It's *burned*," whispered Alice. She didn't have to see the label. A shudder slid over her skin. She was no longer a visitor in her body. She left Mother gazing after her, and went slowly among the boxes in the hall. She lifted the schoolbag, and shut herself in her room.

She squatted on the bed, fearful, surrounded by duckling wallpaper.

Alice – perched on her bed – began to feel cold. She rubbed her arms, and stretched, grinning suddenly, deciding not to be silly.

She wished she had tidied her room sooner because it was looking quite pretty. The window-sill needed painting, but there was no time now. The tip of a postcard stuck up from the row of books on her chest of drawers. She pulled it free and read the neatly drawn writing. *Dear Blobby,* "Pig," said Alice cheerfully. *No talent here. Dragged round this great boring house packed with tea and doughnuts – me, I mean. Animals are terrif and parents speaking to each other. See you Sat. Anne.*

Alice realized the postcard had been shuffled around her carpet since summer. She turned it over. On the postcard was a photograph of a leopard.

"Oh, well," she said heartily, "time for homework."

She pushed the card back among the books and found her English jotter in her schoolbag. She rummaged for a pen, leapt onto the bed and opened the jotter.

She read the essay question.

She read it again.

She read it a third time, but still didn't know what it said. She looked at the row of books beside her on the chest of drawers. The edge of the card peeped out between the spines of paperbacks.

"Even Anne," Alice told herself, "would not call that a coincidence. I mean, a leopard on a card that arrived five months ago, hardly coincides with a leopard in the loft today! Now do your homework."

But she sat, her thoughts heavy on her eyebrows. Then she sighed because there was really nothing to think about. Then the jotter and pen landed on the floor and Alice thudded down the stairs and, sitting among boxes, dialled Anne's number.

"Can you come over?"

"Hang on."

Alice heard yelling.

"After I've done my homework. You'd better do yours, so I don't get flung out early."

It was dark when Alice tucked her books into her schoolbag. From her window the street lights hung in yellow globes of dropping snowflakes. She was pleased the wind had died in case Anne was forbidden to come, for her mother was a creature of sudden demands and illogical terror. One fear was that Anne would blow over and crack her skull, for Anne was tiny and thinly structured, a child verging on adolescence, but built it seemed, of matchsticks and baggy jumpers. Alice had been called "ripe" by a boy in the third form. Under the street lights, she saw Anne.

Anne kicking through the snow, past the corner bungalow, nimble as a kitten, but leisurely, stooping, scooping up a snowball, sending it soaring to plop down into the white road.

She saw Alice and waved. Alice waved back, and Anne danced, scarecrow arms, a staggering twirl, laughing, silent in the distance, plodding closer, dipping again – hand cutting a lump from the cotton-soft ground, and she stopped, still bent. Alice frowned.

Deep in her scarf, Anne's little head tilted as if listening. She straightened cautiously and faced one way into the falling flakes, then turned as if she were as fragile as her mother believed, and faced the other way. A hedge beside her sagged under its top-load of snow. Anne peered, trying to see over, then her face flashed pale in the street-light as her head jerked, then she leapt, knees flickering out of her coat as she ran, cutting a track towards Alice's front door.

"What's wrong with her!" gasped Alice, and raced down to the hall. She jerked open the front door letting light fall out onto the path and the wooden gate.

"What's wrong!" she yelled gently, and Anne fumbled the catch with sheepskin paws, shoved the gate open, scraping a bare fan on the path, rammed the gate shut again. And she leaned over it, looking up the road, like a sailor checking the wake of his ship. Then she turned, cheeks red on white skin, and tried smiling as she approached through the tumbling flakes.

"Hi!" she said.

Alice slammed the door behind them. Anne un-wound her scarf and sprang snow from its yellow length, then sat on a box with FRAGILE inked on its top, and jerked off her wellingtons.

"Hi!" she said again.

The door to the living room opened. "Hello, Anne," said Alice's mother. "Thought it was you. Can you stay to tea? Bit makeshift –" She raised her eyebrows at the boxes. "– but it will fill a space."

"Thanks, Mrs Mason. Oh, my mum sent choco-lates." Anne handed over her snowy coat. "In the pocket. She says to tell you she appreciated your feeding me and putting up with me and doesn't

15

know where she'll send me for peace when you leave. I don't think I was supposed to say all that."

"I don't suppose you were," said Mother faintly. "Say, 'Thank you' to your mother for me, and you can visit us whenever you like once we move. Oh, give me your scarf and wellingtons. The house is sold you know, and we don't want to leave stained carpets. Dad will be here in twenty minutes," she told Alice.

"It's snowing," said Alice.

"Oh," said her mother, and disappeared with Anne's wet clothes.

"Come on up," said Alice. "The electric heater's on. We can make toast. I pinched a couple of slices of brown bread and the peanut butter. Dad's bound to be late, so grub'll be ages. What were you running for? You looked really scared. I didn't see anything."

They tumbled into Alice's bedroom and Anne knelt at the heat warming her palms, turning her miniature hands until the backs were done, then Alice presented a fork with a slice of dangling bread and Anne toasted that like a third hand, then she did the second slice while Alice spread the first with peanut butter, thick as your finger.

Anne shivered as she ate. Alice munched patiently.

"There was something," said Anne, and her fair old-lady curls bobbed as her face turned to Alice, "but . . ."

"But," said Alice firmly.

"I don't know."

"You must know!"

16

"Well. It probably wasn't anything." She bent towards her peanut toast, and Alice waited in silent demand, watching the corner of her friend's snack vanish upwards behind the curls, then appear downwards minus a bite.

"What did you get," said Alice, "for that last algebra equation?"

"X equals six."

"I got thirty-seven and a bit," groaned Alice.

Anne's bright elfin face came up. "I was scared," she said quietly. "I don't understand. There was no noise. Except me. Laughing, and scuffing my wellies. And it's not really dark with the street lights and the snow. But I felt there was something watching me. And beside your house is a big shadow. I nearly went home." Her voice rose in wonder. "So empty looking, down the side where your fence is. I nearly went home. I swerved right across the road. Then your hall light came on and you called and it was all right."

She sat still for a moment, panting slightly inside her fluffy jumper.

Alice went to the window. She pushed the last corner of her toast between her lips and sucked off the peanut butter. Snow fell steadily. Anne's tracks were soft dents, already white. Alice saw where her friend had swerved away from the house. For some reason she remembered the coat.

"We found a coat," she said.

"*Found* a coat!"

"In the loft. It was Grandma Parker's. I'll let you see it."

"I've seen a coat!"

17

Something Watching

"This is special," said Alice, and though her voice sounded cheerful to herself, her heart beat fast and her glance slid away from her friend. She wasn't sure — when it came to the moment — whether she could even touch it.

THREE

"Mum!" she called from the top of the stairs. "She makes me go down," she told Anne. "Hang on."

Down she went, into the kitchen with steam watering the window and Mother peering through half-moon spectacles at a cookery book.

"I'll never get used to these." Mother removed the specs and glared at them. "If I've hit my shins on those boxes once –! Things leap up at me! I hope I don't fall down the stairs –"

"What's for grub?" asked Alice.

"Well. . . The cauliflower soup's good."

"Yug."

"And a quiche. With bacon. You know, Alice, when we move, money will be short. A vegetable garden will be part of your duties, and we'll both have to learn to cook. Maybe I should open a tin," she sighed. "There's so much to do."

"Your baking's improved, Mum," Alice reminded her. "Can I show Anne the coat? Where is it?"

"Hanging on our wardrobe door." Mother wrinkled her eyes at the book then fumbled her spectacle legs under her hair. "I thought it needed airing. It really made me shiver when I tried it on."

Alice retreated upstairs.

"It's in here," she said, and Anne stepped aside letting Alice open the door and click the light switch. "Oh!" said Alice.

"What is it?"

"I saw something move. On the floor. It went

behind the bed."

"A cat I expect. Pussy!" cried Anne.

"I don't know. Soon see." Alice strode across the room with Anne at her elbow.

"Is that the coat!" said Anne.

The coat was on the carpet by the bed. Above it, a coat-hanger dangled from the wardrobe door.

"It must have fallen," said Alice. She lifted the coat and spread it on the bed. She rubbed her fingertips together. Touching it hadn't been so bad. Nor so good. Mum had removed the label.

"No cat," said Anne, her face under the bed. She stood up. "Maybe you saw the coat drop as you opened the door."

Alice shrugged. "It seemed to dart across the carpet. Oh, well. What do you think?"

They looked at the coat.

"It's beautiful," said Anne.

"Yes."

"It's horrid." She grasped Alice's fingers. "Let's go through."

They went through slowly, facing the bed where the coat lay, stepping backwards, flicking the switch, snapping the door shut.

Tight.

A car engine roared. Alice and Anne ran to the bedroom window and looked down. The red blaze of car tail-lights shone from beside the house, turning snowflakes pink. Dark patterns of tyres decorated the drive.

"It's my dad," said Alice, and they rushed down the stairs, bumping, giggling, warning Mother in the kitchen, opening the front door, leaning out into the thickly falling night, seeing the red glow vanish, CLUNK of a car door, SWOOSH and CLATTER of the garage door, and a tall shape, lean, hunched against the weather, merrily stepping towards them –

"Hello, lovelies! Smelly night for driving, but beautiful! Meg," he said, as Mother came, shutting steam in the kitchen. "Had to dig myself out this side of the roundabout. Good thing I took the spade." He hugged the girls and kissed his wife, and Alice smiled as Anne reached up to him and pressed her mouth to his cheek. Alice didn't mind. She knew many parents had no time for their children, and Anne's mum and dad were too busy either screaming or not speaking, to love her properly; though they did care.

"I'm starving!" gasped Father.

"Richard!" said Alice sternly. "You know you don't speak like that!" They giggled, and were horribly punished by having to set the table while Mother and Dad investigated smells in the kitchen.

The chat and laughter continued through the meal (which Mother apologized for, though it wasn't at all bad) and they listened open-mouthed (when they weren't chewing) to Dad describing the castle, but they simply couldn't capture its plan in their heads, though they squirmed with delight, and passed around glances that said, "Did you hear *that!*" and nudged and shouldered in excitement. Anne's face was entranced, saw Alice, her eyes filled with blue sparkles of delight.

At last Father touched his mouth with his

napkin, gave orders to the troops, and in no time the table was cleared, and in rather longer than no time, the dishes sort of washed, and Father with much groaning returned to the garage and transported boxes within boxes, and black bin-bags in a roll.

Alice showed Anne how to place dishes with scrunched up newspaper tucked all round, just so, into the boxes, with handles not touching, and spouts with empty air around them then they surely wouldn't break! and how to list on the outside of the box, what was inside, or unpacking would be a nightmare.

They forgot to mention that Anne had run in a curve through the snow. They forgot completely that Alice thought something had moved along the carpet. And they thought not at all of the coat lying so still and cool across the quilt on her parents' bed.

FOUR

When the clock above the gas fire said *nine*, Anne looked at Alice shyly, and they washed hands slowly in the kitchen sink, frothing bubbles, grey with ink from newspaper. Snow rushed down steadily, creeping up the black glass of the window, shocking them with its relentless descent. The phone rang.

Father's voice. "Mrs Lane. What a surprise. Yes, it is deep. Yes. More than welcome. No, it's not far, but these days . . . kids . . . Yes. No trouble, she can go to school with Alice— Oh? That'll cheer them up. Oh, yes, very busy packing. Yes. Goodbye. Bye."

Alice's hands were cooling in the grey bubbles. She slid a glance at Anne and Anne's mouth opened, and her tiny pink tongue touched her lower lip. She raised her eyebrows and the kitchen door opened.

"You can stay. No school tomorrow." The door shut.

Alice opened her mouth. A yell came out. Hands flashed, rinsing, rough drying, through to the living room where Mother sat in a sea of newspaper, Father reaching for the Sellotape.

"No school?" yelled Alice.

"Forecast's bad. The headmaster's secretary phoned somebody and asked them to pass the word."

"Yippee! And Anne can stay the night?"

23

Calm nods from a busy father.

The girls hugged each other. "Come on," said Alice, and they huddled secretly into the kitchen and quietly, without the least clink of cups or spoons – the bread knife whispering through a loaf, snipping tomatoes, cleaving slices from a block of meat dropped cautiously from its tin – supper. Surprise for the parents, who smiled, stopped to wash black hands, relaxed by the gas fire, Father rising to stroll to the window, wondering out loud if he'd get to work in the morning, and once, glancing at the ceiling as something bumped gently, but Mother said, "Snow off the roof," and no one thought any more about it.

They shared the bed, Alice and Anne, whispers splitting into giggles; eventually shushing each other, for Mother and Dad were asleep in their own room across the landing.

Alice had left the electric fire on. By its red glow, they discussed the snow heaping into layers from the silent sky, thickening gardens, fattening roads, softening the whole world.

Then Anne was breathing steadily, face relaxed with a smile on her elfin lips. Alice rose carefully and switched off the fire. She opened the curtains, then lay in bed.

The yellow luminance of the street lights filled the window. Snow fell, indifferent, it seemed, to the confusion of cars in the morning, or the shovelling of paths by children free of school.

Alice smiled, and snuggled close to Anne, eyes shut, darkness in her head.

*　　　*　　　*

Something Watching

Feet pattered on the stairs.

Alice opened her eyes. She turned her head, and held her breath. The sound had ceased almost immediately. She relaxed, eyes open.

Could there be a cat? Of course. If she wasn't imagining things, there had to be a cat.

Well, afraid of cats, she was not. She eased out of bed and went to the door. For a moment she listened. She didn't want to waken the parents, so pulling her face tight she turned the handle and stepped out.

Downstairs, the glow of the street light turned the red carpet black. Boxes had crept onto the lower steps, square and neat with shiny-taped tops and solid shadows. Alice found the light switch and snipped on the light in the hall below. The boxes all shifted as their shadows darted out of the glare, but nothing really moved.

No cat.

Down she went. Alice. In her nightie, round arms, still brown she noticed with summer tan, into the hall and the stillness of waiting cardboard and drunken black bags. She went among them, seeing the doors shut, to the kitchen, living room, bathroom, Dad's study.

There was nothing. She returned to bed, and slept.

Breakfast was a smell of bacon, and the crackle of knives on toast in the bulb-lit kitchen – for the sun had slept in, leaving the window dark.

Father came clumping through the back door, snow slipping from his wellingtons. "It's no use," he announced. "Even if I clear the drive, there's a good ten inches on the road. We'll make the most of today, and get plenty of packing done. Volunteers to go to the shops for more boxes? You and you! No groans," he ordered and Alice and Anne laughed through their groans, because they really were delighted with the idea of giant plunging steps and stinging cheeks.

"We'll take the sledge!" cried Alice.

"Good idea!" said Dad.

"I'll give you a shopping list," said Mother, and Alice really groaned for she hated being questioned about change when she didn't remember prices.

So packed with food and packed in coats, Anne in her sheepy paws and yellow scarf, Alice a purse buttoned in a pocket, and both dragging the sledge, they stumbled out of the little estate with its soft white bungalows, and along pavements that led among shops, sparklingly lit as night brightened into morning.

They prodded around counters, seeking just the correct loaf, the perfect potatoes, carrots, just two onions (because there were some still in the house), tinned tomatoes, peppers (green), oregano, and on and on.

They asked politely for boxes, and shop by shop, staggering in their wellingtons through such snow! they built the little sledge higher and higher with a cardboard castle and weighed it down with shopping, tied it round as tight as snow-wet gloves would allow.

They found a slope on the way home, and risked perching Anne, light and wobbling on the hastening sledge, with Alice trudging alongside crying, "Hold on!" and "Don't lean over!" until a garden wall swung before them and *bump*, Anne jerked onto the padded ground screaming and laughing, and yelling that her skull was broken. They were out of breath, hot in their clothes, fingers wet, cheeks and noses chilled scarlet.

They approached the house.

Their chatter ceased, breathlessly, faces towards home.

Snow on the roof ripped, exposing red tiles, a lump whumping onto the ground.

The girls paused.

Anne was looking at the house, and Alice looked too, remembering she would see it only a few more times. Mum's pretty curtains. The garage door seemed very green against the snowy ground. In the garden little trees waited for spring, but brittle now in the cold light.

Around the house stood a shadow. Not the shadow *of* anything, just a shadow, a grey ghost blending with the snow.

Alice shivered.

Anne stood close to her, staring up solemnly. "It was there yesterday," she said and Alice didn't have to ask what she meant.

"It's nothing!" said Alice. "Come on!" And they went forward, cool now after standing, up the driveway, round to the back door, sledge lines over footprints, bursting into the kitchen!

FIVE

They burst into silence.

The kind of silence that falls heavy during a quarrel.

Alice's grin became a gape. Anne stepped behind her, tiny and unobtrusive. Seconds lingered as Mother faced the dishes in the sink and Father's scowl blinked into puzzlement.

"Dad?" breathed Alice. She had never seen them like this. Rows happened now and then. But here was real fury. "Da-ad?"

"Oh, I'm sorry!" whispered Father. "Meg." He was beside her and she turned into his arms. "All about nothing," he gasped. "My goodness." He noticed Anne. "Don't be embarrassed," he said, patting Mother's back. "Coffee all round! Yes? Kettle volunteer? Cup volunteer!"

"I'm washing cups!" said Mother and smiled damply.

"Right! Unload the sledge, you huskies! Wellies off! Coats off! Grinning from ear to ear! Sorry!" he whispered again to Mother.

"Come on!" cried Alice. She looked at her father and he smiled feebly. She dropped her wet woolly fingers onto a radiator and attacked the castle on the sledge.

In two minutes the huskies were tumbling fresh doughnuts from a baker's bag, and a score of new empty boxes blocked the hall. The kettle whistled that water was ready. Mother had cups and plates ready, and Father clattered a spoon around the coffee jar. Hot coffee and doughnuts had never gone down so well, and chatter – once Mother's smile was genuine, not just pretence at being happy – the chatter sparkled like snow in sunlight. Then during a pause, when there was much munching, and catching of jam on chins, Mother mentioned the coat.

"But where is it?" she asked.

"Let's not start again," said Father gently.

"I'm sorry, Dick, but I would like to know! It couldn't just disappear!"

"All right!" cried Daddy, obviously determined not to loose the cheerful mood. "The jury will be sworn in!" He stood up, thumbs in waistcoat, though he wasn't wearing a waistcoat. "Alice Mason, do-you-swear-to-tell-the-truth-the-whole-truth-and-nothing-but-the-truth?"

"I do!"

"Place your right hand on your doughnut!"

Screams of laughter.

"I do!" shrieked Alice.

"Do you, Anne Lane, swear-to-tell-the-truth-the-whole-truth-and-nothing-but-the-truth?"

"I do!" squeaked Anne, swearing on her plate, because her doughnut was eaten.

"I do! I do!" protested Mother.

"Miss Mason, when did you last see the item in question?"

"We left it on your bed!" cried Alice. "Last night."

Suddenly it wasn't funny.

"I hung it back on its hanger on the wardrobe

door," stated Mother. "Alice—"

"It was on the floor, and I lifted it onto your bed. I only touched it once." She added, "Maybe that's what ran down the stairs."

Three faces took her seriously. Mother sighed, her hair as soft and dark as Alice's. Father sat down. Anne's fingers closed on Alice's arm.

"I just thought," said Alice, "that I heard feet on the stairs during the night. Like a cat. Only heavier." She shook her head. "But there wasn't a cat. Nothing." She beamed at the rest of the jury.

"Well, then," said Father at last, "we've been burgled. Someone popped in – through the back door – ah – up the stairs . . . took the coat . . . um . . ."

"It's hardly likely," said Mother, "with me in the kitchen almost every minute of the day. More coffee?"

"No. Yes, please."

Alice slid off her stool. "Yes please to coffee."

She went through the hall, heaving aside boxes, up to her parents' bedroom. She shivered a little, glancing out to the winter landscape. Bungalows stood snug in white jackets. The coat-hanger hung on the wardrobe door. She opened the wardrobe fully. The animal shape of the coat was asleep on the wardrobe's floor. Alice smiled with one corner of her mouth, and shook her head at parents everywhere. She returned to the kitchen and started on her coffee.

"It's in the wardrobe," she said wearily, "on the floor."

Mother jumped, then hurried out. They heard

her feet quick on the stairs. They waited. Her feet descended, heavy on each step as if she were thinking. She stood in the kitchen.

"I don't understand," she said.

"Drink your coffee," said Father kindly.

"I looked and looked." She sat at her cup.

"My parents fight all the time," said Anne, and everyone stared at her. "I like coming here."

"We like having you, dear," said Mother. She turned to her husband. "Dick, I'm sure it wasn't in the wardrobe."

SIX

Alice, Anne and Father took the coat to the auction – hand in hand – so no one would fall.

The auction room had two vast windows on low window-sills. GEORGE MARTIN, AUCTIONEER, EST. 1895 curved in gold lettering across one window. The lower three-quarters of each window was painted on the inside with brown paint.

"What's the point of windows you can't see through!" squeaked Anne.

"In we go," said Father. "Got the coat?"

Alice waved the coat in its carrier bag.

Glass doors shut behind them.

"Well!" said Father.

"Oh!" cried Anne and broke free.

Alice hooked the carrier handle onto Father's fingers, and stepped into a wooden city.

Its streets were gaps between wobbly buildings made of stacked furniture. Chairs were heaped at impossible angles. Wardrobes showed mirrors where girls hid. Bare bulbs gazed at floorboards.

Alice and Anne wandered, trailing fingers. Father found them. Without the coat.

"How much did we get for it?" asked Alice, relieved.

"We'll have to wait till it's auctioned, but the woman thought it might be valuable."

"What'll you buy me?"

"We'll get you something in the thick-ear shop," said Father solemnly.

"Ho," said Alice, which was half a laugh. Anne giggled, and they followed Father, but Alice stopped him.

"Where is it?" she said.

"The coat? In the office. She'll pin a number on it and display it. If you can call this 'display'."

"Do you know that Grandma Parker wanted it burned?"

Father stared. Anne stepped closer to Alice.

"What d'you mean?" said Father.

"There was a label. It said, 'This coat must be burned'."

"I shouldn't think—"

"Why were you so bad-tempered about it? It's a beastly thing, Dad. It really gave me the creeps."

"Well. It's gone now. And we'll get some good hard cash. Let's explore. You know, we could do worse than buy furniture here. We'll need to fill the castle somehow. Look at that. That's split, but a bit of glue. . . Either of you two got a pen? What's the time? We don't need to be home for a while. Thanks Anne. And a bit of paper." Daddy fished inside his wallet for paper. "Right. Here's the drill. See the numbers on the larger stickers? Make a note of anything that catches your eye."

"What about these little numbers?" said Anne.

"These represent the owners. You might find a small number – five, say – on several things, so they all belong to owner five. But there's a large number for each item. So. . . Now, look here, piglets. I'll need your help. Chances are, I'll be back at work tomorrow so if we get this done now. . . You think like this: What are we going to need?

33

What will look good cleaned up and in a castle? Remember the walls are plaster or wood-panelled, not wallpapered or bare stones ... Well, some bare stones. Ceilings are higher than at home. Is this too much for you?" Shaking of heads. "Remember, if it's broken, it may sell cheaply, so if you think I can repair it ... You get the idea ...?"

"We'll need another pen," said Alice.

"Right. You take the pen, and go along this whole ..."

"Street."

"Yes. I'll get a pen at the office and start elsewhere. Watch out for woodworm!"

"Do they bite?" asked Anne, when he had gone.

"Of course not! I don't know! Let's start. What a lot of junk!"

"This is nice."

"What's the number?"

They learned. Alice found it strange that her brain changed its thinking. Instead of believing everything was just old and boring, she found her eyes searching beneath the dust, seeing that quaint little chair gleaming – with her own carpet under its lion-clawed feet. And this table with the leg knocked straight and its sun-bleached top rubbed to a rich bloom by Father's lean fingers. And that pair of vases, gigantic and repulsive if you thought of them in a modern house – but see them as sentinels on either side of an oak doorway, and their bulk is suddenly *right* and the crawling detail perfect against a stone wall.

As they worked, the bulbs high in the roof

gradually brightened, and shadows deepened full
of jutting bony limbs which were chair arms and
table legs. Dark glitters of glass blinked from
bookcases, and the children giggled less among
that mountainous furniture, and their chatter
faded into the pointing of a finger, a nod of the
head, and a careful gyration of the pen.

They moved on. Deeper into this endless city.
Round a towering corner, searching, seeing occa-
sionally another citizen, but absorbed, noticing
each other just enough to let them squeeze past.

It seemed that a shadow fell across them.

Alice looked up, expecting an end of a rolled-up
carpet, or *something*, blocking a bulb. But there
was nothing; just the bare underside of the roof
and the row of lights.

Anne, buried head-first to her waist among chair
legs, wriggled free, dirt on her cheek, curls dancing
as she jerked to look this way, to peer that. Then
she too glanced up, and went close to Alice, and
the silence continued, cold pressure on Alice's palm
as Anne's fingers gripped in fearfully.

"Say a prayer!" whispered Anne.

"There's nothing—"

"Our Father . . ." Anne's eyes shut, and her lips
wriggled rapidly. Alice saw the fingers of her free
hand were crossed to keep the darkness away.

Alice said nothing, but stood with her friend,
wondering if Dad was nearby. She recalled the
shadow around their house, wondering if prayer
might not be a bad idea.

"Oh, come on," she said, *tick tack.*

Anne's eyes jumped open. Her fingers bit Alice's

palm. *Tick tack* said the shadows.

"It all creaks," whispered Alice. "It's been creaking since we came in. Everybody knows that—"

Tick-tack, tick-tack.

They shuffled. Anne tugged. "It's got claws!"

Alice gritted her teeth and found her lips pulled back in a silent snarl. Her heart hit a double beat and her legs were strong down to the floor. But her brain sat cool behind her eyes; eyes watching, brown and beautiful that third form boy had told her. How absurd to think on boys just now! *Tick tack.*

They moved backwards.

"We must get on," said Alice as firmly as she could. "There's lots to look at—"

Something slid, pale and straight, slanting from the shadows, striking the floor, *bump* flapping a small coloured wing, and they rushed, still backwards into the furniture, and stopped, Alice not letting Anne go, saying, "It's only a map! Look. A school map rolled up!" Its coloured wing was merely the map's corner uncurling, flickering New Zealand at them, printed red.

Little Anne was panting, and Alice's heartbeat was a deep thump and the pen and paper were wet with sweat in her fist. Alice stepped forward freeing herself from Anne's fingers. She said, "That sideboard—"

Tick tack!

Alice twirled at scuttling feet. She was alone, Anne's wellingtons fleeing around the corner.

High up, something moved. A stool on its back,

short legs like a dead bug, but the stool crept on
its fabric back, towards the edge of its perch, *being
moved* thought Alice. Then the table supporting
the stool leaned out over Alice, and the stool
leapt –

Alice jumped. She fled, clattering after Anne,
hearing the crash of tumbling furniture, fleeing
from fear, heaving open the glass doors, stopping
on the pavement among people.

They looked in through the open door.

A woman stared out, not unfriendly. "Was that
you?"

"It just fell," said Alice. "It nearly landed on
me."

"It happens. Are you with Mr . . . Mason?"

They nodded.

"Don't go away. I'll tell him you're outside."
The door shut, and they breathed.

It was getting dark.

SEVEN

The roads were clear of snow the day Alice and Mother and Dad moved house. The little bungalow seemed stacked to the ceiling with boxes, and extra furniture picked from the auction room. In the hall, you had to walk sideways, and on the stairs – oh, the stairs were almost hopeless, but Alice thought her parents did well, clambering like jolly spiders. Not that everything for the castle was packed into the bungalow. Wardrobes waited for them at the auction room, and tables and carpets, the giant vases that Alice had chosen, and many other exciting things, but even all that, Father had said would only fill a little bit of the place. It would take years, he told Alice cheerfully, years and years of buying, repairing, polishing, to put the castle in order.

But they were on their way.

Buzzing along in the car, Alice in the front, Mother in the back, balancing cups to feed the workers.

It wasn't too far at eighty miles an hour, and not much further when a lorry slowed them to forty; and pretty close, when the road shrank to a lane and Alice thought Dad was crawling to tease her, but the lanes were confusing like a broken ball of string, and signposts at junctions pointed across fields, or into somebody's pigsty.

It really wasn't much further when Mother recognized a church tower, though where the road had gone to that led there, nobody knew.

They drove out from the cold brown fields, and the smell of the sea hit them. The church and its village straggled behind. Trees before them, stripped naked by winter, seemed to bow in welcome, but really were brushed by sea winds into permanent stooping. Beyond the trees, lay the castle.

Out they got, slowly.

Stepping onto gravel worn into the earth. Glass sparkled as if someone had washed the windows specially. The castle stood ankle-deep in neat strips of garden, so dainty! and no more than one storey high – except above the door which was built into a little keep full of odd windows. Alice couldn't tell if it was two storeys or three. Battlements just big enough for children to defend, wandered along the tops of walls.

"But it's tiny!" cried Alice, her breath white in the frosty air.

"It's not Caernarvon," grinned Father.

"Wait till you see inside!" said Mother.

"And round the back," murmured Father jingling keys.

"Look," said Mother, nodding, and beyond grassy ground bumpy with hummocks, a cottage sat, surrounded by its garden; windows hooded in thatch, glittering as if they'd been washed specially. Smoke from the chimneys rose tall into the sky. On the grey water, small as a matchbox, lay a ship.

"It's all perfect!" gasped Alice. "Richard," she said proudly, shaking her father's hand, "well done. Well done, old chap! Wait till Annie sees this! She'll be green!"

She snatched the key and ran to the door, astonished at its vastness now she was close, searching the keyhole with the iron key. It was quite as wide as the garage door at home – at their last house – and higher, curved to fit under the stone arch, solid with oak and iron studs.

The key clunked, and Alice pushed. Father's hand reached past her grasping the handle, and pulled.

In the ground under Alice's feet was a curve of metal, and as Father pulled, the door swung, rolling on the metal rail, and inside – Alice grinned with delight – for inside was not the inside at all. The gravel flowed under the arch and faded into a courtyard encircled by the rear windows of the castle, and by stables and out-buildings. Towards the sea, a stone wall was the boundary, broad enough to stroll on, though tumble-down, with a couple of turrets, and its top solid with grass.

"I hope the removal men don't get lost," said Mother.

Father nosed the car through the archway, and began unloading the boot.

Under the archway, at her right, Alice found two doors, and on the facing wall, on her left, the real front door with a foxface brass knocker.

So in they went, arms full of things too precious to leave to the men, into a hall with angled walls rich with wood-panelling. Coloured daylight blazed softly down a curve of stairs – coloured, because the stair windows were decorated with stained-glass coats-of-arms. Goblins' heads gazed from every corner. A fireplace waited for Christmas. Tiles clicked under Mother's heels.

"It's fantastic!" said Alice.

"Dick, couldn't we light a fire! It's so cold."

"I'll do it!"

"Do you know how?" asked Father.

"Coal and a match!"

"Wood and a match. And kindling."

"What's kindling?"

"Something that will light easily. Dry paper, twigs. . . Don't you want to see the rest of the castle?" Father sounded disappointed.

"Of course I do! I'm saving it up. Bit by bit. Any matches?"

"You hunt up the logs," said Father. "I saw a stack in the courtyard last time I was here. I'll leave matches on the mantelpiece. Off you go."

"See if the removal van's coming!" cried Mother, as Alice, bursting with excitement, went in search of something to burn.

EIGHT

Alice stood under the arch. She looked out to the front of the castle with its neat gardens below the windows, the trees with their hair brushed by the wind, and the cottage, sparkling at her from under its bushy brows of thatch.

She tried the doors opposite the front door. One was locked, the other let her into a toilet with a spider-clogged window and a wooden seat. An old-fashioned chain had a china handle printed with the word PULL, and Alice obliged, surprised when the ancient cistern flushed with a great gush of water.

She went into the courtyard. Something glinted on a large door. She didn't investigate, but stood, holding down her excitement, gazing around.

Beyond the tumble-down wall peeped the ridge of a glass roof, so she crossed the courtyard – discovering cobbles among the weeds – and clambered onto the wall, walking on its grassy top. The courtyard was on one hand, and a rocky shore slid down to the water, on the other.

She used the wall as a path, finding her way around one of the little turrets, peeking inside but seeing just rubble and gloom.

She turned the corner away from the sea, towards the cottage with its friendly purl of smoke. Beneath her, leaning against the outside of the castle wall, was the hothouse. The glass of its roof rose at Alice's feet, green with frozen slime.

She climbed down a buttress into the courtyard and found a wide opening in the wall. She had seen the opening, of course, but it didn't do to acknowledge everything at once. Bit by bit. On the far side of the opening, nearer the castle, was the door with the glint.

The glint was a padlock; freezing in her fingers, and quite locked. "Locked tight," said Alice, and a ring rattled on a window. Alice turned and eventually found Daddy grinning and waving. She waved back, and he rubbed his shoulders, shivering like a bad actor, reminding Alice that she was hunting logs.

She found them stacked against a wall, snow in their crevices, sawn short enough to fit the fireplace. She managed to lift three but one fell, and she ran. She put the logs in the hearth and had to search again for kindling. Dry straw from the stables burned faster than she expected, and it took quite an armful – plus a wooden tomato box which she broke up – stuffed into the nest of the fireplace, flamed with a match, pouring smoke – to light the logs. But she did it.

Alice sat, her hip on the hearth, shivering, smiling fatly at light draining through the coats-of-arms in the windows. Not so happy about the goblins' heads.

She rose, rubbing her cold cheek, and walked along a passage with panelling carved like hanging cloth; then into a long room that split her smile wide at the fine panels on the walls and ceiling. More heads listened to her footsteps.

She ran to an inglenook with a stone fireplace, then dashed to a second fireplace at the other end of the oak floor – then to the window-seats where a lady could view the approach to her castle.

A door creaked and Father sauntered grandly, then grabbed her, and they danced along another passage, with windows peeping into the courtyard. Alice glimpsed the padlock.

Into a kitchen.

"Oh, great!" said Alice, and Mother smiled, for the kitchen was hot.

Mother was beaming almost as fatly as Alice. "It's practically new!" she said, pointing at cupboards and the cooker and neat shelves. "And look at this!" And *this* was a giant stove with the word Aga on it, with hot-plates on top, and doors in its front, and bright yellow like an enormous hot canary, for the stove shimmered with heat. "It was on when we came in," said Mother. "Daddy didn't arrange for anyone –?"

Father's head shook and he handed Alice a cup of milky coffee which she guzzled as she poked around, peering out the window to the padlock. This was the window Daddy had waved from pretending he was cold. The ship was gone from the sea, or perhaps was hidden by one of the turrets on the ruined wall. Beside the window was a door to the courtyard.

She heard a *peep-peep* and the nose of a removal van crept through the gap beyond the padlock. "They've found us!" cried Alice.

Father said, "Ah," jibbled his coffee, and ran.

*   *   *

Something Watching

The men marched in, laden with boxes from the chalet bungalow.

The bungalow seemed part of a different life already, to Alice, pointing out where her bed should go in the little room she had chosen; chosen for its thick brown central heating radiator and many shelves behind cupboard doors that rose to a ceiling so low that she could reach up without stretching and touch its rather plain panels.

The men carrying her furniture grinned, bending through the doorway and staying bent until leaving then straightening with exaggerated groans in the passageway.

"It's a linen cupboard," explained Alice. "My room's actually a linen cupboard."

It was dusk when the men left.

"Well, that cost me a tenner," said Father in the kitchen, as he opened a box marked GRUB and lifted out tins for Mother to heat.

"Is that all?" said Alice.

"Tip," explained Father. "A tip to protect our new antiques and the woodwork. Isn't – it – marvellous! Hello? Did you hear a knock, just then? What about this tinned pie? What's this? mung beans? What's a mung bean? No jokes, thank you, about what a mung's been. I'm sure I heard a knock."

"I'll go," said Alice.

She went.

To the hall with the staircase, searching for a light switch, *click*, the brass switch chilly on her palm, the front door facing her, silence, now the light was lit.

NINE

The smell hit Alice when she opened the door. Hot with flavours. In the light spreading from the hall, large spectacles shone, and a smile.

The spectacles advanced bearing the smell before them. "Are you in the kitchen?" asked the smile, and strode through, hands huge in oven gloves, holding a dish made of pottery, green as sunlit grass, still burping under its lid. "What's your name?" The voice was light, with a country burr, as warm as stew to Alice.

"Alice."

"I see you've got the fire lit. It'll go out with the logs like that," and she strode to the fireplace and kicked the logs so they lay parallel and flames leapt with delight. "Open the doors, then," she said. Alice followed her to the kitchen where she brushed through, dumping her pot of smells on the Aga.

"Melanie," she said, dropping the oven gloves. She pulled off her glasses and laughed. "I'm all steamed up!"

"Mrs Mason," said Mother. "Meg Mason. Dick —"

"Blessings." Melanie wiped her glasses on her apron, put them on and smiled.

She was quite beautiful.

Thin-face, bony wrists jutting from a jumper as thick as a carpet, long hands, fine like an artist's. Teeth slightly long, and white, her cheeks creasing to give the smile room, slight lines at her eyes vanishing as her face relaxed, and her hair silvery fair and heavy enough to swing at her jaw. The apron strings nipped tight around her waist.

Father hurriedly stood up.

Melanie's hands produced paper plates and plastic forks from her apron pocket. "You can throw these away when you're done. I know what it's like, moving in. Can't find nothing except your bikini or the lawnmower or some such useless jimjams."

"It's very kind of you . . ." Mother, still with the tinned pie in her hand and her half-moon specs on, hesitated.

"Now you eat your supper while it's hot. Rabbit stew. You'll be partial to rabbit? Good. And fresh vegetables out the garden. Well, out the freezer." She turned to Father. "You won't have the central heating going yet? You just follow me – he won't be long, my dear. There's a trick to starting it. A good kick on the third join . . ."

They faded into the house. Mother and Alice looked at each other and exploded with laughter.

"Who is she!" cried Mother.

Alice shrugged cheerfully and headed for the stew. "I've never tasted rabbit."

"She didn't say where she lived! Oh, that looks delicious! I've found the loaf so we'll have bread – Oh, good, there's potato in it."

Mother slopped the stew from the dish onto plates, because there was no ladle; down into tummies; groans of delight.

Father returned and joined in, offering Melanie

a share, but her head shook, sparkling her hair, and it seemed to Alice as she slowed down shovelling the stew, and took time to look – to feel around with her mind – that their visitor was special.

Energy, thought Alice, billowed from her; not just in the chatter, not in the quick graceful steps or dancing fingers; not just in the tightness of her muscles or the merriness of her smile, but somehow, radiating, glowing around her, warming the space where she lived. Melanie.

"Where do you live?" asked Alice. "In the cottage?"

"That's right. Me and my Jack." Her smile widened. "Jack's the grave-digger –" Mother's mouth hung open. "– for Impney, Long Common, Bishop's St Mary, and here, of course. The nearest graveyard –" She gathered them close with her fingers and her eyes stretched wide behind her glasses. "– is there!" And one finger pointed suddenly at the kitchen wall.

"In our pantry?" asked Father.

"No, silly!" She laughed. "But you're not far wrong. Didn't you see them hummocks between you and me? It's not just rock like the shore, you know. The soil's deep. I reckon it must've been forest once, and those trees, stiff with the wind, are what's left. And those hummocks are what's left of a proper graveyard. Cavaliers and Roundheads. I know. I looked it up. Though it ain't used now, of course."

"Any ghosts?" said Alice. Then – for some reason – she remembered the coat, and wished she hadn't asked.

"Ghosts? Why no, not that I've ever seen. Though there's plenty of power if . . ."

"Power?" said Father into his stew.

"If what?" asked Alice.

"Well . . ." said Melanie cheerfully. "Just power. Lot of bitterness in them days, you know. Bitterness is power. Still there, waiting to get used. Now poor Meg –" Melanie reached across the table and prodded Mother's shoulder. "– is looking very serious –"

"I really don't believe . . ."

"Believing don't change what's there," said Melanie. "Now, you're all looking tired. I'll leave you to it –"

"Did you light the Aga?" asked Mother. "And clean the windows?"

"Did it between us, my dear. You want anything, give me a shout. You want a hand with knocking down," she told Father, "or building up, my Jack'll help. Or digging," she grinned. "He's good at digging. I'll go out this door. Thought I'd use the front door for my first visit."

Then they went to bed, Alice, glad that tomorrow was Saturday and Anne was coming. Glad that the radiator gurgled, promising warmth, for the linen cupboard was cold and slightly damp.

TEN

Alice opened her eyes. She had spread her soft coat on the bed for extra warmth and its collar was over her mouth. She pushed the covers aside.

Daylight hung in the little room. Alice picked her way bare-legged among unpacked belongings, and gazed out the window.

Over the lowest dips in the tumble-down wall, the sea lay dark as steel and great shovelfuls of cloud packed the sky. Clouds full of snow, thought Alice with delight, and her smile spread, for Anne would arrive early to stay the weekend. The padlock glinted mischievously. Then she danced on one foot wondering where the nearest loo was.

Breakfast in the kitchen, with tea, and toast lumped with marmalade but no butter because Mother hadn't found it; and fresh scrambled eggs, because she had found eggs – "On the window-sill!" she exclaimed. "I had to wash the straw off them!"

"We've chosen good neighbours," said Father. "The Aga's marvellous!" he beamed, touching the hot canary. "Stayed on all night. We'll have to be economical, you know. Shutting doors to keep the heat in. Planting vegetables."

"Chopping wood," said Mother.

"We might get chickens," said Father finishing his froth of eggs. "That was good."

"And a cow!" cried Alice.

"And a farmer to look after it!" cried Father.

They laughed, and Father explained how money would be spent on replacing broken tiles on the roof, and preservative for the timbers in the attics; some might need replacing; glass fibre to roll out between the rafters to keep heat in the rooms below; paint for windowframes, especially those facing the sea . . .

So they planned, Alice chatting madly, but wanting also to explore, for she hadn't been in every room. She wanted to see everything, touch, embrace even, the ancient ramparts of this new home, making it truly home, for she loved it already.

She said, "What's the time? Annie should be here!" She raced, then walked pompously in the long room then raced again as a car stopped.

She leaned on the great oak door beneath the arch, to push it wide.

"A present for you!" yelled Anne.

"Thanks!"

"It's homework. English, French, maths and geography."

Alice groaned.

"You shouldn't take days off, Blobby. This is a real present for your Mum and Dad."

"Housewarming," explained Anne's father. "I'll just say 'Hello' and be off."

When he left, Alice and Anne explored, thrilled at every corner. Up the staircase in the keep, above the hall with the fireplace, they found an absolutely perfect room with windows which opened onto the battlements. "This," giggled Alice, "will be my lady's very own private sitting room!"

At lunch time, the van appeared, nosing into the courtyard, dropping a flap at the back, unloading furniture. Items needing repair went into the stables. Everything else was directed by Father to its correct place in the castle. Alice and Anne helped. More or less.

Father frowned over another tip. "We'll send the bill, Mr Mason." Hands were washed, and sighs sent out over Melanie's (very-late-in-the-afternoon) reheated rabbit.

Then after eating (Alice and Anne bulging with tinned rice pudding) they puzzled over the padlocked coach house. No key could be found, and no time wasted hunting, for there was unpacking to do, cleaning to do, polishing to do, lying exhausted to do, not to mention stoking fires, shovelling coal for the Aga – (They found a vast hoard of coal in a laundry room through the door that wasn't the toilet door, under the archway.) – adding up receipts for the furniture from the auction room (Dad's job), finding more food in the chaos and making it edible (Mother's job), trying to locate the orchard mentioned in the lawyer's letter so long ago and not succeeding –!

For a rest, Alice and Anne decided to visit Melanie. They took her grass-bright pot, thoroughly scrubbed by Anne who loved pottery, over the lumps in the graveyard, up the straight path of a garden well-tended, though in its winter sleep. They pressed the bell and were yelled at merrily not to stand on the doorstep as if they were visiting but to come in as friends should.

So they went in as friends, through to the
kitchen, after stepping mistakenly into a parlour
and shyly retreating. Melanie welcomed them,
thanking them for the pot, and they thanked her
for the stew, and she promised more, but meantime
made tea and hot scones which they managed very
well despite being tight with pudding.

Alice asked about the padlock.

"Oh, that's mine," said Melanie. "That's my
pottery. I don't use it weekends during the winter,
and of course, not yesterday with you moving in—"

She stopped. "Oh, my! I never thought! It
belongs to you now, doesn't it? Fancy that. Well,
I'll need to make other arrangements. Your dad
must've been puzzled finding the coach house
locked against him. Well. I don't know."

"Your own pottery!" cried Anne.

"I made that." Melanie's fingers took the children's glance to the stew pot. She laughed. "And
all the others, come to think of it. Mr Gray let me
use the coach house. Being the biggest building
available, you see, and me turning out so much
stuff and him not running a car no more, so not
requiring a garage. Your dad'll need it for his car,
won't he? I can't think . . ."

"I'm sure he'll let you have some space," said
Alice. "I'll see to it. I'll bully him."

"Don't you go troubling your father. He'll have
enough —"

Melanie's smile stopped being a smile. The
kitchen, thought Alice, was filled with her warmth.
She sat still as if listening.

"I can't hear anything," said Anne.

Melanie looked at Anne through her large glasses.

"Oh, I'm not listening, my dear." She stood up carefully. She went to the window, which faced the sea. Again she stood still. She turned to Alice. "You in trouble?"

Alice glanced at Anne who raised her eyebrows.

"No," said Alice. "What do you mean?"

"There's something not right," said Melanie quietly. "Come with me."

She led them to the parlour, where again she stood at the window, gazing at the brushed trees; but not listening.

The heaped grey sky dropped a snowflake on the garden. More snowflakes, fat and lazy, ambled down, resting on the cold ground.

Melanie moved quickly out of the parlour, out the front door, her apron tight around her waist, snowflakes on her hair. Down the path, swiftly, Alice and Anne puzzling along at her back. She stepped onto a mound in the graveyard, straight as a young tree, unheeding of the cold, searching in a way Alice could not understand.

Melanie's head turned, half towards the children, mainly towards the castle. Her beautiful face was solemn and the eyes behind the spectacles saw nothing, nothing – thought Alice – in this world.

Then her voice cried thinly into the monstrous sky, and she rushed at the girls, gathering them with her, making them run towards the cottage, up the path, slamming the door on the dropping soft day, into the heat of the kitchen. And she sat at the table, trembling.

Terrified.

ELEVEN

The girls stood uncertainly, then Melanie tidied away the tea things, but only, decided Alice, for something to do. A tremendous frown burdened her face. "Perhaps it's not so bad," she muttered, and looked at Alice. "Perhaps it's not so bad. My Jack says I exaggerate, and there's always balancing power. We forget that in our fear, don't we?" She smiled.

Alice blinked. "We don't understand. Why did you go rushing about? I mean—"

"Oh, don't pay no attention." Her smile slackened. "It's just my game."

Silence.

Then a bright flash of teeth and spectacles. "I've got a present for you. Both of you. Just stay here. Have another scone." She left.

Anne tilted her elfin face. "What a funny lady!" she whispered.

"What was she on about! Some game! She was scared."

"She's cuckoo!" hissed Anne. "Living over a graveyard would make anybody silly. But I like her," she added.

"She is different."

"Your dad fancies her."

"Hah! How do you know!"

"Kept mentioning her."

"Midget."

"Blobby."

As they exchanged insults Melanie returned with little linen bags throttled by coloured raffia. She hung one round each available neck. "And that's for your mum and that for your dad. There! Make sure they wear them. Now, pop back any time my dears, but you must excuse me as I've got a meal to prepare. Digging's hungry work, you know!"

Snow fell, thick and slow, turning the castle into a ghost of itself.

"Look!" cried Alice. "From these trees, across to the graveyard –" She made a rushing, bumping motion with her palm.

"Let's," nodded Anne, and they dashed through the bombarding air, into the castle courtyard, rattled the padlock in punishment for being mysterious, found the correct stable door, and inside, the sledge resting its nose on a wall. Furniture from the auction sat around like patients at the dentist's.

"I like this chair," said Anne.

"Don't bounce on it! The leg's split. Gosh," said Alice, "Dad's got a lot of repairing to do. What's wrong with this? Oh, that's not bad. Look at the crack here –"

"I want to sledge," said Anne. "Before it's dark."

"Come on then!"

Off they went, two huskies, barking outrageously, fat flakes on their tongues, sledge lines wending in the graveyard, cutting the snow in front of Melanie's cottage. Bumping up the slope to the trees.

"Isn't it great!" yelled Alice.

"Yes! Turn the sledge! Me first! You push!"

"Y'say, 'Mush'."

"Mush! Mush!" Anne sprawled on the sledge, face down, reins tight, and her husky pushed –

"Hooray! Good husky!" And the good husky tumbled on top of Anne, determined not to be left. The sledge fled, just fast enough up-a-bump down-a-dip, heading for a hummock, the air full of screams, whooshing to a stop. Then again! hauling the sledge, snow filling the huskies' hair, filling the creases in their sleeves.

The girls' cheeks brightened, breath whitened, noses glowed, and shoulders gathered cloaks of snow. Darkness crept between the trees, brightening the castle lights and a lamp on the corner of the cottage wall. The graveyard loomed in the dusk.

The man came from the lane. Silently, his cap solidly white, hands deep in his coat pockets, but striding cheerfully.

"Hello!" he cried, and the girls stood still.

"You must be Alice." His face, now he was close enough to be seen, was round and weather-beaten, and his smile went up at one side. He was quite ugly, decided Alice, but she grinned because he was nice, and she knew he was Melanie's Jack.

"Who's this?" asked Jack. "Your sister?"

"No. This is Anne. She's staying the weekend."

"She'll be staying longer than that, if she's far to go," smiled Jack his eyebrows indicating the weather.

"Have you been digging graves?" said Anne.

"That's right. And hard work it is at this time

of year. Though I've seen it frozen a foot'n'more deep, and it's not that bad yet. Come January, perhaps. You need a pick for that. You enjoying your new home?"

"Yes, thank you."

"You call me 'Jack'. Everybody does. From here to Impney, I'm Jack the Gravedigger. Well, see you soon — what have you got there?" He stared at Alice then at Anne. "Did my Melanie give you these?"

Alice touched her linen bag.

His smile had melted, but he wasn't annoyed, just serious.

Alice nodded.

"What did she tell you?"

"What do you mean?"

"About wearing these herbs."

"Nothing really." Alice looked at Anne.

"Nothing," said Anne, "but she rushed us into the cottage."

"She didn't say nothing?"

"No."

"I see. Well. Don't get them too wet." He smiled again. "My belly thinks my throat's cut." He strode away.

"He looked awfully serious," said Anne when the cottage door had closed on Jack.

"She didn't even say it was herbs." Alice sniffed the little bag. "Let's go in."

They pulled the sledge towards the gap in the castle wall, returning it to drain in the stable. They jumped to knock snow off their clothes, then they ran, beginning to chill now, into the kitchen, to heat, and Dad's angry gaze.

"Hello you two."

"What's wrong?" Alice pulled off her anorak, and put an arm around his neck.

"The auction people," said Mother, her nose busy in a pot on the Aga.

"What is wrong," said Father grimly, "is that I phoned the auction room to see if the coat sold – to see how much it made. Do you know how much it made? Not a thousand pounds. Not five hundred. Not even one hundred." Father tightened his lips. "Nothing!" he muttered.

"Nothing!" said Alice.

"Nothing. They put my name in the book. They put a number on the coat. They hung it up –"

Alice opened her mouth.

"It vanished," said Father.

TWELVE

Alice stared out from behind her eyes. Her breath slid up and down in her chest. It was this strange feeling again, of being a visitor in her own body. As if Alice Mason and Alice Mason's body were two different things. She was sure that with a little effort she could step away and leave her flesh hanging on her bones.

She saw Father as if he were no longer her dad, but an actor on a film. She heard the clink of a fork on the Aga and the whisper of Mother's clothes, and the rubbery hollow clunk as Anne removed her wellingtons.

"You don't think the auction woman would keep it for herself?" said Dad's voice a great distance away.

"She'd never be able to wear it, Dick. A coat like that –"

"Oh, I know. Alice. Are you in there?" He waved, and Alice filled her body again, shivering.

"I'm sorry I'm bad-tempered," said Father. "Same as the other time that coat . . ."

His lean face was serious, then he pushed out a smile. "Oh, well. I was only going to say, 'the other time that coat disappeared'. I don't suppose it makes a habit of it. Is it colder in here? The Aga's hot enough, eh? You two won't be cold? Saw you sledging. Was that Jack, talking to you? I thought he'd've had a long shovel over his shoulder and a mad gleam in his eye. What's he like?"

"Nice," said Alice.

"And ugly," said Anne. She went close to Father for a hug.

"Oh, that's kind," cried Father. "Ugly. Haven't you two got slippers or something? Alice, are you all right?"

Alice wondered if – when this strange feeling came again – if it came again – she wondered if she dared take one little step . . .

She beamed at Daddy and he grinned tugging her cheek. "Go on," he said. "There's a utility room through there – half a dozen of 'em in fact! Wellies and wet things. Then slippers. Homework . . ."

Double groans.

"After grub, Richard," said Alice.

"After grub," agreed Richard, and they bundled clothes and wellingtons into the utility where pulleys creaked down from the ceiling to take wet things, and hot fat pipes wormed low along the walls, heating the air. Then a mad dash on slate floors, feet skidding in socks, along corridors, under a roof full of beams, oak goblins grinning at passing humans . . .

Bursting into the linen cupboard.

"It's freezing!" yelled Anne.

"No, it's not. The central heating's on. We'll light the fire."

"But we'll have to go back out for wood!"

"There's plenty in the hall."

Racing, still slipperless, over ancient floors, stealing logs from beside the blaze in the hall, and staggering – "Mind the panelling!" – with pieces of dead trees. Elbowing door handles, bottoms pushing doors, discovering (with their hands helpless) that doors opened outwards into the corridors rather than inwards as at home – at the bungalow.

Then the fire was lit, and a fireguard imprisoned sparks, and slippers warmed feet. Places were chosen for doing homework. They made a game, Alice and Anne, of getting books and jotters ready. There seemed no point, Alice felt, in mentioning her strange sensation of being separate from her body. Anne wouldn't understand. Even Dad . . .

A gong boomed stupidly and they laughed and found a lunatic drumming the gong in a passage near the kitchen. They rushed into the lunatic and he grabbed them hoisting Anne clear of the floor dragging mad Alice screaming to the kitchen, where the lunatic turned into Father and they sat panting over soup plates, craning towards the Aga to spy on the main course.

"What about insurance?" asked Mother.

"Not a hope," gasped Father. "They say they couldn't possibly insure everything that came into the auction room. How could they put a value on things? If somebody walks off with a thousand-pound coat – hard luck. On us. Anyway, the woman told the police, and anyone wearing it –"

Anne was nudging Alice.

"What are you up to, you mice?" asked Father.

"Melanie's presents," said Anne.

"Right!" said Alice, rising –

"Not just now, darling," said Mother. "The chips are nearly ready. Eat your soup. Oh, there's so much to do!"

"Now don't worry, Meg. There's lots to do, but all the time we want, to do it in. The main thing is that the heating is working and we have a supply of logs and there are boxes and boxes of food. Well . . ." he explained to the girls, "I thought I'd buy up a load in the supermarket and bring it with us. I knew we'd be too busy to go shopping – and look at that snow!"

The early evening stood black beyond the window. Snowflakes slid down the glass.

Alice looked at Anne, and Anne's elfin smile flickered.

"You do your homework anyway," said Father reading their thoughts, "whether or not there is school on Monday. And what's this about a present?"

"One of these," said Alice, lifting the linen bag at her throat.

"Very generous."

"I think it's a charm."

"Ah."

"She was odd," said Alice and they told Father and Mother about Melanie, with lots of interruptions, and "No, she didn't" and "Yes, she did" and gigglings and snortings and sighing after laughter.

Then Alice, resting her fork on her fish fingers, remembered the strangeness of Melanie in the graveyard and her terrible cry in the winter air, and her own shock when she heard that the coat had vanished. She said, "I was a bit frightened." Then they talked of other things, Father recalling jobs to be done.

"I must check the roof tomorrow," he told his

wife, and was immediately bullied into taking two inspectors with him, to supervise.

Then the meal was finished and the inspectors avoided washing up by claiming that homework waited. They dashed to the linen cupboard, stacked another log on the fire and settled to business.

The fire made most noise, roaring at the children from the safety of its nest, then lying silent until "kicked like a dead dog" as Anne said, to see if it could be roused.

They tested each other at French vocab. Anne helped Alice with maths. Alice worked determinedly.

"Where's your *Minty's English Grammar*?" asked Anne.

Alice waved at the cupboard once used to store bed linen. She fingered her calculator, ignoring the click of the cupboard door, the slither of the book from between its neighbours.

"Oh," said Anne, "here's that postcard I sent you last summer. 'Dear Blobby . . .'" She giggled. "'No talent here, blah, blah, blah. See you soon.' What rubbish."

Alice tightened her lips.

The card dropped onto her jotter.

She pushed it aside, writing.

Anne sat down.

Alice glanced at the card.

She dropped her pen.

She pushed herself back from the table. Her jotter skidded to the floor taking the card with it.

"What's wrong?" said Anne.

Something Watching

Alice stared. She remembered Mother in the bungalow unfolding the coat from its box, the tissue paper dropping.

She pressed her back against the cupboard, to keep the shudders away.

THIRTEEN

"Alice what is it!"

"Get Daddy!" whispered Alice.

"But what's wrong!"

"*Get Daddy!*"

Alice pumped her fingers open and shut. She rocked against the cupboard door. She stared at the card on the carpet.

She listened to Anne's feet running through the castle. She heard her voice piercing the corridors.

Father's steps came heavily, and Mummy's voice, into the linen cupboard –

"Alice!" Father, shocked at her rocking.

He held her pumping fingers and she shrank against him, shivering in his arms, Mother's touch on her back.

"What happened!" demanded Father.

"I don't know!" cried Anne. "She was working and jumped away! Something scared her."

"Are you ill?" asked Mother, staring around the linen cupboard. She lifted the postcard and jotter, tidying them onto the table.

Alice shivered and stood free of Father.

"D'you want to tell us?" said Father.

"Do you remember the night," whispered Alice, "that Anne stayed with us in the bungalow? Because of the snow?"

"Worked like a soldier," said Father. He sat on Alice's bed because his head was bent beneath the ceiling's wooden panels.

Something Watching

"Before Annie came, I found that postcard –"

Anne lifted the card, and handed it to Father. Mother squinted over it, without her half-moon spectacles.

"– and I felt . . . shivery."

"I don't see . . ."

"*Daddy!*" Panic in Alice's chest. "Daddy, I sat holding that card, reading it, looking at the leopard –"

Father frowned.

"– telling myself it wasn't really a coincidence that Mum had found the leopard-skin coat . . ." She stared at her mother. "You tried the coat on, didn't you?"

"Yes . . ."

Alice imagined the coat folded into tissue paper inside its flat box with Grandma Parker's name on the outside, and the box lying in the attic of the chalet bungalow – waiting.

"I think you woke something."

"But it's a giraffe," said Anne. "I remember sending four or five cards, all giraffes –"

"Alice," said Father gently, "What –?"

"It was a leopard. On the card was a photograph of a leopard."

"Then it was a different card," said Father. "Really –"

" 'Dear Blobby'," said Alice firmly. The others stared at the card. " 'No talent here. Dragged round this boring house –' "

" 'great boring house'," mouthed Anne.

" '– packed with tea and doughnuts – me I mean. Animals terrif. Parents speaking to each other. See

67

you Sat. Anne.'"

The fire whimpered.

Father placed the card on the table. He took his hand away carefully.

"But there *must* be another card." He looked at Anne.

"I only sent one," she said reasonably. She sat close to Father on the bed.

Mother took a breath to speak, and everyone looked at her; but her lips closed, and she blinked.

"Well." Father looked at the card. "You couldn't have thought it was a leopard, I mean . . ."

The picture stared up at them, spindle-legged, neck like a drain pipe.

"So what made you think up a leopard?" asked Anne.

"I didn't think it up –"

"The card didn't change," said Anne. "Did it?"

"I don't know! No! No. Of course not."

"Then it was just your imagination," announced Mother. "Are you all right now, Alice?"

"Oh, *I'm* all right." Alice put her hand flat on the card to prove she wasn't afraid. The fire whispered secrets to the hearth. "But something is free, Daddy."

"Alice –" said Father in his reasonable voice.

"Didn't I find the coat in the wardrobe, after Mum had searched there?"

"Alice –"

"And didn't you go into a real fury, Daddy? About nothing? You never do that. Then we took the coat to the auction."

"Something creaked," said Anne. "Up among the furniture. Like claws tick-tacking –"

"And it's disappeared again," said Alice. "From the auction room. Now there's a shadow over the castle, just as there was a shadow over the bungalow. That's what Melanie felt, when she stood in the graveyard. Even before we knew the coat had come back."

"Come back?" mouthed Mother.

"It came from the auction room in the last load of furniture," said Alice. "Must've done."

FOURTEEN

Alice faced Father on the bed. "Was the coat Grandma Parker's?"

"Yes. Alice, this is crazy –"

"Tell us about her."

"Tell us," pleaded Anne.

Father thought.

"There *was* something. Meg, do you remember? She mentioned the coat in her last African letter. Oh, yes. It was odd because she talked about the coat in the same letter that she told us about Grandfather Parker's murder–"

"Murder!" cried Anne.

"He was a policeman," said Alice.

"In Nigeria," explained Father. "Somebody shot him – though they'd tried other methods to get rid of him. Mumbo jumbo. You know. He was good at his job, and a lot of thieves wanted him out of the way. He told us some strange stories –"

"What about the coat, Dad?"

"When Grandma wrote with the news that Grandfather was dead, she said that the coat had appeared in the house – if I remember correctly – on the morning of the day he was killed. She couldn't find out who it belonged to, so it seemed sensible to bring it home to England. I think she had to pack it herself for none of the black servants would touch it. I'd forgotten that," said Father to himself.

*　　　*　　　*

Tick tack.

Had she dreamed it?

Alice opened her eyes. Darkness stared down.

Her fingers found the bag at her throat.

A flicker of flame lit the hearth.

Tick tack padded in the passageway.

Alice pushed Anne's firm little shoulder, getting a sigh out of her. Push again.

Tick tack, naturally quiet as a cat is quiet, not sneaking, *tick tack*.

"Anne!" Alice gave a savage little push.

"Mm."

"Listen. Listen!"

Anne's eyes opened.

The fire puttered.

Alice slid from the bed, feet into slippers, touching the ceiling for balance.

"What is it?" whispered in the firelight.

"Something in the corridor."

"Your dad going to bed."

"Listen!"

"I don't hear anything!" Anne was under the covers.

"Get up!"

Alice hauled on a jumper. "Get up!" she ordered.

She found a shoe and gripped it like a club, but it weighed almost nothing.

Anne shivered into her dressing-gown. "It's that noise we heard in the auction room!" she gasped.

"It's that beastly coat," said Alice.

"Rubbish!" A hysterical shriek.

Alice turned the door handle, pushing the door

just wide enough to see the pale square of a window.

She looked round the door. Panelled walls stood in darkness.

Something gleamed, small as an eye. Anne's fingers touched Alice's back. Alice brushed the wall with her palm striking the light switch.

There was nothing.

"Come on!" Alice went forward.

"Why are you not scared?" hissed Anne huddling close. "You were scared of the postcard."

"Shut up. I didn't understand the postcard."

"You understand this!"

"If it makes a noise with its feet then it's real. Ssh!"

They edged round a bend in the corridor. Shadows swallowed its length.

Alice snipped on another light, doors gaping –

"You go that way –"

"No!"

"All right. We'll look in each room."

"Waken your dad."

"No. Not yet. Shush now. This door." She pulled the handle, feeling the awkwardness of doors that opened outwards.

She found a switch but there was no bulb, just the flex dangling in snowlight from the window. A single table stood helpless in the middle of the floor. There was no other furniture, and nothing moved.

They searched, shivering with cold and nerves. Furniture shoved approximately into place left nasty corners to peep into, and wardrobes made high dark dens for crouching shadows. Mirrors startled the girls. Then they shivered more, and agreed that it was much too cold to go on hunting, and they crept away, switching off lights, shutting doors to keep in heat they couldn't feel, hurrying in the corridors, not hearing the *tick tack*, kicking the dead dog into life, placing the table across the door (forgetting that it opened outwards), lying with the light on, trying to sleep, trying to stay awake . . .

Air hung cold in the linen cupboard.

Pale light, bright for the early hour, inspected dust on the wood-panelling, gazed at the jumble of Alice's clothes and the folded pile of Anne's. It puzzled around the bulb still lit, and the table blocking the doorway. Alice smiled. Then she remembered the *tick tack*.

She leapt up, yelling at Anne, kicking the fire hopefully, though only ash was left. She hauled on jeans as she hobbled to the window.

Weeds in the courtyard wore hoods of snow. Outbuildings stood under thick white roofs. Melanie's cottage was hidden by the stables but Alice saw smoke puffing from its chimneys. And the sea was a strip of lead. Alice pushed aside the heaviness in her mind.

"I'm putting on two pairs of socks!" she said and dug in her chest of drawers. "Get up!"

Anne crept shivering, into her clothes.

"Do you think that horrid thing's still around?"

"We'll soon find out! After breakfast we'll search every corner. You know, there are rooms I haven't seen yet! What's the matter?"

"What if we find it?"

Alice squeezed her sock-fattened feet into slippers and made a firm little smile. "Race you to the loo!" she said, and fled, thudding on the oak floors.

They found a loo each, then rushed to the kitchen.

The kitchen was cool.

"We're first up," said Anne.

"So we are," said Alice. "Shovel some coal into the Aga and open the vent. I'll do the breakfast."

The kitchen filled with clattering, as dishes and cutlery appeared. The frying pan warmed its bottom on the hot canary, and smells followed as toast was burnt in the cooker's grill and bacon sparked and eggs turned from liquid to white, staring at the ceiling with yellow eyes.

"Where are these parents!" complained Alice. "They'll be late for school!" Laughter, and shifting the frying pan from the heat, boiling the kettle. "I'll give them a knock. You watch the grub. Dad likes ketchup."

She went towards her parents' room, touching radiators to feel their heat, wondering where the intruder was, but not frightened exactly. Her insides surged with. . . Oh, she didn't know what. Energy. Confidence. She smiled at the panelled walls. Fear perhaps. She thought of the countryside, soft and silent, split by smoke from Melanie's chimneys – and the fresh trickle from the Aga's flue.

Knock, knock.

Something Watching

"Mum. Dad. You awake? Daddy?"

She pulled the door.

Her mother was sprawled on the bed, very still, her eyes open. Daddy was half-way between the bed and the door, curled into a ball, cold and motionless on the carpet.

FIFTEEN

Panic.

Alice couldn't move fast enough.

She threw herself on her father, screaming. Then at her mother screaming, screaming, panic, shaking the limp body, clutching her mother's head. "Mummy! Mummy!" Beat at Father, pummelling his arms with her fists, his back, her screams ringing around the ceiling, shivering on the glass in the cold windows, howling along the corridor, her throat on fire with the noise, half blind with tears, terrible strength in her body, hauling Father upright, demented energy as she gripped him under the arms and lifted him to his feet, but he folded onto her and they fell, utter screaming as Anne's hands reached to help, Father flopping, but he breathed –

"Keep him moving!" she bellowed and flew at her mother dragging her from the bed, half catching her, half letting her drop to shock her to life, her screams deliberate now close in her mother's ear, shaking her whole body, slapping her arms slapping her face till her skin reddened and Mother's eyes blinked slap! moan slap! slap! a yelp from Mother, a vast hug in Alice's arms, tugging, proper colour in Mother's face and breathing, real breathing –

"Alice," from Father.

"Dad!"

"Oh." He caught Anne feebly. "You can stop

76

shaking me. Meg!"

"She's coming round. Dad!" His arms embraced Alice limply.

"Meg!" he crawled and collapsed. Mother lay looking at him, not trying to speak. He crawled again, Alice helping, screams, it seemed, still ringing around the ceiling, though only weeping from Alice and Anne; weeping in terror and relief.

"Melanie," said Alice. She turned to Anne. "Get Melanie!"

Melanie came. Swiftly. Powerful. Freezing Alice's blood with the look on her face as she stared at Father and Mother, motioning silence.

Her voice seemed carried on a distant breeze, startling Alice, making Anne stare.

"The bags of herbs," breathed Melanie. "You were to give them to your mother and father. They protect and restore. Fetch them . . . quickly."

"I don't know where they are!"

"I'll look," cried Anne and she returned soon. "They were in your pocket in the utility room."

"Place them around their necks."

Mother and Father lay on the floor, blankets warming them, conscious, but unmoving. Melanie watching all around them it seemed, through her large glasses, examining something Alice could not see.

Then she said, "He is well."

Father sighed, and a weary smile announced he was better.

"And Meg," said Melanie. Mother's eyes moved, and she struggled to sit up.

"I'm black and blue," moaned Mother.

"We can leave them now," breathed Melanie, "to dress."

"Shouldn't we get the doctor?" whispered Alice.

"No," drifted into Alice's mind. "They will eat."

Father sighed, leaning back from a well-scraped plate. "Best rubber eggs I ever tasted. You can stop looking at me like that," he told Alice. "Won't you sit down?" he asked Melanie for the third time.

But Melanie's hair swung pale, as she shook her head.

Mother was eating.

"Tell me what happened."

Alice stared as Melanie spoke. What *was* so strange about her?

"Well," said Father. He looked at Mother. "Well. It sounds silly in daylight."

"Go on."

"Oh, a virus!" said Mother. "I've had something like it before . . ."

Father's hand covered Mother's fingers. "No, Meg." His fingers trembled. "There's a shadow over the castle. There was a feather –"

He released Mother's hand, letting her eat, "– jagging me. Here." He put his hand on his solar plexus. "It got so annoying, I put the light on and looked at the sheet. I couldn't see a feather, but the jagging went on. I felt as if something was being pulled out of my stomach. Then Meg –" Mother stared at her plate. "– she got restless. There was no way we could sleep. It went on for hours, then I realized Meg wasn't moving. I felt the life had run out of me. I couldn't stand. I crawled, hoping to waken the children . . ."

A sob rose in Alice's chest.

"I get the impression," said Father to Melanie, he patted Alice's fingers and she held tight, "I get the impression that you know what's happening?"

Melanie's silver-blonde head flashed as she looked at Alice. Alice looked back, seeing blue eyes, beautiful behind the glasses, full of wisdom. Then Melanie's glance went to Anne, Mother then Father.

Melanie didn't speak, and they waited.

Alice gripped Father's fingers. She felt Melanie's presence – not just as a person – but filling the kitchen with comfort and protection.

Father was staring at Melanie as if he sensed it too, and his throat moved as he swallowed. Mother sent her fingers creeping to join Father's hand in Alice's.

Anne sat, wide-eyed, a smile born on her elfin lips, her little back straight and joyful.

Tingles of delight sprinkled down Alice's skin and she knew that these moments were magical; and the moments grew, building into joy that threatened to float her to the ceiling. She felt this so vividly that for a moment she saw nothing, heard nothing, felt nothing but bliss. Then it lessened, and she relaxed, staring around the kitchen. The fingers in her grasp tightened as Mother and Dad stared too.

"Melanie's gone!" said Anne.

SIXTEEN

Father murmured, "She must have slipped away."

Alice remembered the shadow over their bungalow in the snow. She saw again, Melanie, slim as
a young tree, crying to the heavens above the
graveyard. She remembered herself, standing inside
her own body, certain that she could walk out of
her flesh. She thought of Melanie, just now, so
strange, as if a dream of Melanie had become
real . . .

The only sound was the murmur of the Aga, the
shift of a sleeve.

Brief little smiles were thrown from face to face.
Peace filled the air like summer roses. No need for
words. Just breathe the silence. Feel the harmony.
Bathe in the calm. It was like – thought Alice –
being in the arms of a mother who could never
die. Her tears of terror over Mother and Father,
became tears of happiness trickling to meet her
smile. Even Father's eyes were moist.

At last they moved. The table was cleared,
washing up completed, the Aga wiped lovingly,
coal bucketed and carried by two happy girls,
poured into the little wooden bunker.

The universe was complete. There was no doubt
about the perfection of things. With a castle one
storey high beneath snow-filled ramparts; with the
flat sea no one need ever cross; with the courtyard
and countryside . . .

"And good things to do," said Father quietly,

and everyone knew what he meant.

Mother wandered into the corridors with polish and a duster, still murmuring about a virus, but singing in her throat.

Father took the inspectors into the attics, discovering, in the exquisite room in the keep, a door which looked like a cupboard door, but when Alice pulled it open, they walked into the triangular world of timber and plaster beneath the castle roof.

They stepped from beam to beam, well warned not to step elsewhere or they would crash through the ceilings of the rooms below. Father's torch reached the darkest places and the girls stared into its yellow exposure of black timber and dust, not knowing what they were looking for.

Father pointed out tiny holes on a beam under a skylight. "Woodworm," he explained. "I've got something in a can that'll make their eyes water."

"Just think," murmured Anne. "In a hundred years parents will come up here and show their children the old twentieth-century repairs."

On they went, entering dark caverns, creeping around a brick column that Father said was a chimney. Feeling small beneath massive timbers. Walking, now, on proper floorboards, meeting a stone wall splashed with light from Father's torch.

"We'll need to go back," he said. "Hello?"

"A door," said Alice.

Father tugged. The door creaked and daylight squeezed around the door into the attic, not bright, but enough to dazzle them.

The doorway was blocked by dark lines with shapes on them.

"Shelves," said Father. "Ah." He lifted a shape and handed it to Alice, who passed it to Anne, who replaced it on the shelf. "Pots. This must be Melanie's store room. Above the coach house – the pottery."

"Can't we get in?" asked Alice.

"Not without breaking down the shelves."

"Or squeezing between them," said Anne.

"You, maybe," said Father, peering in at an angle. "It's shelved all round. It would be a shame to ask her to move everything out."

"She'll be pleased about that!" Anne pushed her head between the shelves. "What a lot of pots! I can see snow," she said, her head right in the room. "The skylight's broken."

"We'd better tell Melanie," said Alice.

"Let's go," said Father.

Anne took her head from among the pots and stood straight.

Father began to close the door.

Alice stepped aside, taking a last glance around the store room.

Alice leaned against the stone wall as Father shut the door.

She saw the yellow swing of Father's torch.

Deep in her chest, her heart thrust blood too fast through her body.

"You coming?" asked Daddy. The light struck bright on Alice's eyes. "I say, you're not still upset –"

"I'm all right," said Alice. "Can we go downstairs?"

"There's more to see –"

Something Watching

"Please."
"You are a bit ghastly."
"Is the door shut?"
"Yes."
"Hurry, Daddy. Come on, Anne."

SEVENTEEN

"This way!" said Alice, clattering down the stairs from my lady's sitting room, into the log-fired hall.

Daylight lay on the floor tiles, coloured by the stained-glass windows.

"Come on, Dad! Wellies! Come on, Annie!" she cried. But her cheeks sagged anxiously as she ran through the castle to the kitchen, "Hello, Mum!"

"I'm having a break," said Mother over her half-moon spectacles and patting her magazine. "Dick –?"

"We seem to be going out," gasped Father.

"Alice!" said Anne.

"Outdoor gear!" ordered Alice.

Wellingtons bumped as they strode from the utility room, past Mother –

"I'm going for a bath," said Mother firmly, tucking the magazine under her arm.

– outside to the snow. Someone, it seemed had balanced cotton wool on the coach house padlock. The courtyard wall was a long wandering cake, with white icing.

"It's Christmassy," said Anne.

"Christmas!" said Father. "D'you know, I'd forgotten? Christmas. Not a present bought. This is Sunday. Well! Something else to think about. You two can hunt down a tree. We'll use the long room. It's beginning to warm up, and with both fires lit and plenty of furniture. . . We must dig out the decorations . . ."

Something Watching

Alice, striding toward Melanie's cottage, noticed Anne apparently shrinking inside her anorak.

"Anne can stay, can't she?"

"Mm? Oh, yes. If your parents don't mind. Won't they want you at home? No? Sure? Well. We'll speak to Mummy – perhaps she would like to run in to town for Christmas shopping ... Alice, it's almost lunch time. Melanie won't want us trooping—"

Alice turned on Father.

"That thing's in the store room above the pottery!" she hissed.

Jack was bigger than Father. Standing in the doorway, up a step, he was gigantic. He smiled and welcomed them and they kicked the step respectfully before entering, like an Eskimo ritual, but only to shed snow from their boots. They went into the kitchen, Jack ducking under the oak-beam lintel, smells of beef and baking.

"Come in, my dears," said Melanie. "I'm warming the kettle. Meg not with you?"

"Having a bath," said Father. "And reading recipes in her magazine. She's experimenting with vegetables. She reckons we'll eat off the land come summer."

"So you will, Dick. And my Jack'll help turn the soil, and the fruit trees will need a dose of winter tar wash, wouldn't you say, Jack?"

Jack nodded, then told Father that the plum trees and apple and pear trees grew on the far side of the castle, sheltered from the sea but exposed to the sun. "And that John Downie," said Melanie, "makes the best crab-apple jelly, you wouldn't believe!"

The talk ran on, Father glancing at Alice, Alice looking back at him, waiting to speak; Anne drinking tea, eating pie made from apples grown last year in the castle orchard. "Mr Gray," explained Melanie, "let me use as much fruit as I could, just so long as I shared the homebaking. He never went short of jams or home-made wine or fruit pies." She beamed, her beautiful face serene behind her glasses.

"About this morning," said Father.

"Still morning," said Jack. "What about it? Heating conked out?"

"No, no. Just wanted to thank Melanie for her help." Father peered at Melanie. "We didn't notice you leaving." Melanie busied herself with her cup. "You had quite an effect . . ."

"Leaving?" said Jack, as if the word was unfamiliar.

Father nodded, and Alice paid great attention.

"Yes," said Father. "You sound as if you don't know what I mean. When Melanie came over to help Meg and me. Then in the kitchen—"

"Hold on," said Jack. "Hold on, just a moment. Sorry to interrupt, but do you mean *this* morning or—"

"This morning," said Father.

"Well," said Jack, leaning back and lifting his apple pie. "I don't know who visited you this morning, but it wasn't my Melanie." He bit the pie. "She only got out of bed half an hour ago."

EIGHTEEN

Alice saw Jack's round cheeks flicker with muscles as he chewed. Dad's mouth opened, then shut as he searched for a polite way, guessed Alice, of disagreeing. He turned to Melanie for help, but she was pouring tea, though Alice saw her eyebrows lift.

Anne cried, "But she was there!" and Jack's head shook, as if it wasn't worth arguing.

"We all know perfectly well," he replied, "that even Melanie can't be in two places at once –" He was looking at Anne, speaking confidently, the adult telling the child. Then his glance wavered and he swallowed. "Unless . . ." he whispered. "Melanie, what have you been up to? You haven't succeeded? Is that why you lay in?" He stared at her. "You can't have done it!"

Father said, "Anne came here to fetch her."

"Melanie?"

"I met her crossing the graveyard," whispered Anne.

Melanie looked at her husband.

"If you've succeeded," said Jack, "you've gone too far. You've gone too far!"

Melanie stood up. "Have I, Jack? Tell me how I can go too far? When a human being treads the Path to Perfection how can she go too far? You know what I am. You've known since we were children that I could heal your cuts and soothe your tears. You know enough about me not to fear for your own identity because of my powers. Have I ever caused you to feel unworthy? You are my husband and the centre of my life on this earth, but I am what I am. I cannot change even if I would."

She stood close to him. "Does my love suffocate you?" His head moved. "Are you not quite, quite free to be yourself? Do I ask you to lose your skill with the spade? Or your magic touch in the garden? No one but a fool would seek to undo such talent. I cannot dig as you dig, for I am not you. No more can you do what I do, for you are not me, and as your knowledge grows so must mine. As the garden responds to your call, so do the powers within me respond to mine. It is simply time, my Jack, for me to reach this stage."

She held his face in her hands and he nodded, smiling a little, eyes moist. She kissed him on the forehead, and turned to Father, to Alice and Anne.

"I came when you called," she said. "I came swiftly and bathed you with Light. Did I not say, 'He is well' and he was well? Did I not say your Meg was well and she was well? No, I didn't cure you, but your aura was dark and shrunken, for the life had been drawn from you. Then you grew strong under my protection, and your aura shone again. That is how I knew you were well.

"And when you needed me no more did I not vanish away leaving you restored? But know what I am saying. I do not do these things. I am merely the instrument of powers greater then you can understand. This earth is well loved. Could the trees grow without love? Could the clouds climb the sky in such majesty without love? I am merely the channel for that love, and I am humbled and overwhelmed to find that this body is lightened sufficiently to release my astral at your cry. My physical body did stay in bed as Jack told you. What you saw was my astral body, and what you felt was the love that holds the universe together."

Alice understood what Melanie had said about the astral body, for had she not felt exactly the same thing? That she could, with a little effort, step away from herself? *How would I get back?* she thought, and jumped as Melanie faced her sharply.

"What is it?" said Alice.

"You *know!*" said Melanie. She stared at Alice and knelt before her, holding her hands, tears bright behind her glasses. "You do know, don't you? Tell me you know!"

"Yes. I know," whispered Alice. "But how would I get back?"

"Is this a secret?" asked Father. "Or—"

"Hush!" said Melanie warmly. "It *is* a secret! You will always get back as long as the silver cord is not broken —"

"Silver cord?"

"The silver cord is a wonderful mystery, but it joins you to your body. You simply picture yourself back —" Her fingers crushed Alice's hands. "— and you are back! It's that easy!"

For a long moment Alice could not understand her own feelings. This strange ability she had discovered was real.

"What's an aura?" asked Anne.

"An aura?" said Melanie. "Why, it's something

we all have. A glow around our body. You'll have seen it in paintings of saints. Someone sensitive enough can see —"

"There's a thing in your store room," announced Alice. "It's what attacked Mum and Dad."

Melanie stared at Alice.

"We went through the attic," explained Alice. "There's a door behind your shelves. I saw darkness and fur —"

"Fur?" Melanie opened a drawer in the kitchen table and took out a key.

"It's a leopard-skin coat," said Alice. "From Africa."

Father said, "Meg's parents were in Africa. Her father was a policeman. I know it's crazy, but he believed he was under attack from witch doctors. Cost him a fortune in gin to hire better witch doctors —"

"And the coat was brought back?" frowned Melanie.

"It was in the attic for ages," said Alice. "Mum tried it on when we were packing to come here —"

"I've heard of this." The key moved nervously between Melanie's fingers. "The first person to wear the coat would waken the elemental . . ."

"What?" said Alice.

Melanie stared from behind her glasses. "An elemental is a creature of the astral plane. Called up — I suppose — by a witch doctor to kill your grandfather."

"Oh," said Alice.

"Of course!" said Father. "Only it didn't succeed. Someone else shot Grandfather the day the coat appeared . . ."

"He was shot?" said Melanie. "The coat didn't kill him? Then that's why it's here. It has to fulfil its purpose. Even though he is dead it will stay among you trying to destroy him." She looked hard at Father. "Feeding on astral energy."

Anne shrank against Alice.

"And now," breathed Melanie, "it's in my store."

She went out and returned with wellingtons and an anorak. She pulled them on. "I may not be strong enough to deal with this. But you mustn't be afraid. Fear is the greatest enemy. It opens the gates. Come. Come. Everybody!"

They left the warmth of the cottage.

They stepped high through the snow to the courtyard. Melanie knocked snow from the padlock and turned the key. Jack hauled the door until it jammed in the soft ground. They stepped into the coach house. Melanie switched on strip lights. There were no windows.

A grey metal kiln, taller than Alice, stood coldly, waiting to burn clay into ceramic. Alice saw a potter's wheel and paper sacks of clay with numbers stencilled on them. She saw loose boards for carrying pots, and buckets and sieves for glaze . . .

"It's warm when the kiln's on," said Melanie. A shudder almost threw her against Jack. They stood at the foot of a wooden staircase. "It's been here!" she whispered. "Can't you see the shadow!"

"You mean it's not here now?" asked Father.

"Maybe it's gone out the skylight," said Anne. "The glass is broken. I saw a roof tile on the floor —"

"Well," said Father, with a gasp of laughter. "Having to come and go through a window. It must be real. I thought it was some kind of ghost."

"It is a kind of ghost," said Melanie. "But it needs the coat to keep it on the physical plane."

"Ghost?" whispered Anne at Alice's shoulder.

"It can't have got far," said Father rather loudly. "It can't —"

"Dad?"

Father's mouth stayed open, twisting. "Oh!" he whispered. "Meg!"

"Daddy!"

"Come back!" squealed Anne.

"Daddy!"

Alice pounded after her father across the courtyard.

He shouted back at her, "Your mother went for a bath!"

Alice knew that the coat's only exit from the store room was through the skylight and onto the roof.

She raced through the castle to my lady's sitting room in the keep. She hauled open a window and slid onto a snowy walkway.

She ran behind the battlements.

Chimneys stood tall above her, silently smoking.

Paw prints met her in the snow.

The prints left the walkway, dotting up a slope of the roof, and circled a wide brick chimney.

She clambered to the chimney. Snow around the rim was broken. Alice stared down inside. Bricks jutted making steps for small feet. Too small for Alice.

She slid to the walkway, and thudded towards the keep. She fled down the staircase.

She ran grimly in the corridors.

NINETEEN

Whispers of laughter.

Had she really heard it? She stopped running, fingers on a radiator. Panting.

A joyful shriek rang from the kitchen.

"Mum?" breathed Alice, and her face felt its way towards a smile.

Father's voice bellowed.

Alice ran down the kitchen passageway.

She stood straight to ease her breath, then reached for the door handle.

Laughter exploded. Yes, they were all there.

She touched the handle.

She had never heard Mother snigger like that.

Alice frowned.

Little Annie never *cackled* like that!

Alice's frown deepened into a scowl. She withdrew her fingers. She turned, and strode through her castle.

She left by the main entrance and marched across the courtyard to the kitchen window. She glared through the window.

Mother was wearing the coat.

Alice's rage boiled.

She heaved open the kitchen door.

Father turned, tongue bright in the electric light. Alice thrust him backwards off his chair. She grabbed the coat's collar and dragged her mother from her seat – pushed her with strength that staggered Mother into the snow. She hurled Anne against Melanie and Jack, then she was in the courtyard, hauling at a sleeve, freeing her mother's arm, hearing snarls in her own mouth, rolling her mother in the snow as the coat came free.

Alice fled through the gap in the wall, over the mounds of the graveyard – the coat, it seemed, twisting in her grasp – onto rocks on the beach, tripping, rising immediately, racing to the grey water that sucked stones.

She ran into the sea.

She stuffed the coat beneath the surface.

She waded to the beach and lifted the biggest boulder her hands could hold. She heaved it towards the coat. She hurled another. More stones broke the water.

Then she fell, barnacles grazing her arm; freezing up to her thighs; gazing astonished at her wet legs; blood on her jeans from a fall she didn't remember. Wellingtons heavy with water.

Alice limped through winter grass to the graveyard. She smiled fiercely as Dad helped Mother to the kitchen. Melanie and Jack stood dazed. Anne came, begging-armed to Alice.

And Alice stood strong before her castle, snow-flakes on her face.

She raised her mind in triumph.

She had won.

She scarcely remembered the next hour, and had to be told several times that Mother had left her bag of herbs in the bedroom, and when she returned from the bathroom the coat was on the bed.

Of course, thought Mummy, Father had found it. Just as Alice had said, it had got mixed up in the furniture sent from the auction room. She had dressed and slipped the coat on. It really was beautiful . . .

She recalled a nightmare of laughter, and woke from the nightmare to find Daddy helping her up from the snow in the courtyard.

Mother didn't remember taking Father's bag of herbs. When Melanie and Jack had come in, Father had snatched theirs.

"I don't know who took Anne's herbs," whispered Melanie. "But that awful thing was enjoying life through us! Sucking us dry! Forgive my anger! I will pray."

"She prayed!" said Anne. "I'm always telling you to pray. That was why we felt better so quickly!"

"You felt better because your mum said you could stay over Christmas, because there was no school anyway because of the snow –!"

But they did feel better. They heard Jack hammering boards across the store room skylight.

The day passed, snow on snow. Dusk gathered into night. Lights in the castle switched off, and tomorrow . . .

TWENTY

"Open sesame!" cried Alice and little Ali Baba pushed the great arched door, and Alice dragged the sledge, equipped with rope, saw and survival rations – though lunch was not long over – under the arch onto the snowscape in front of the castle.

Melanie's cottage streamed smoke. Jack's footprints – left forgotten as he walked to work hours earlier – were just dimples wending up the track between the trees.

"Follow me," said Alice, and they circled the castle away from the cottage hoping to travel between the shore and the trees.

When they rounded the corner of the castle they found the orchard. "Rows of witches!" cried Anne, and Alice agreed that the fruit trees with their bare black arms and scaly grey coats of lichen, were rather unfriendly.

"They must be cold," she said, but a brick wall protected the orchard from sea winds. The children trailed the sledge to the wall and peered through gaps designed to break the wind's strength. Alice turned away. She didn't want to remember yesterday, wading out to drown the coat, to bomb it with stones . . .

"Come on!" she yelled, and rushed among the witches, the sledge bouncing on the bumpy white ground.

"Mush! Mush!" cried Anne, and they raced along the pure snow, the sea on one side, trees bowing on the other.

"Well, Captain Scott," gasped Alice, "I estimate we'll do a hundred miles today if the huskies don't break a leg."

"Can they keep up this speed, Cap'n?"

"We can't both be Captain!" said Alice.

"If we can both be huskies, we can both be captains!"

"Oh, all right! Onward! Sing out if you see a polar bear!"

"Aye, aye, Captain!"

So the huskies raced on, miles of wasteland dropping behind, hour upon hour of the polar day slipping away.

Quarter of an hour, anyway.

They stopped, panting, the sea grey and wrinkled. Trees crowded down to a stream to drink, and across the stream, beyond the white ribs of a field, sat a farmhouse.

"A polar bear!" cried little Captain Scott.

More trees grew beyond the fields, some spreading their branches to let winter blow through, other draped in green fur coats, their arms drooping to shed snow. Alice said, "That looks promising!"

The polar bear advancing from the farmhouse, scratched its red face with a very large paw, and said, "Hello. Haven't seen you around here?"

"We've come from the castle," said Alice.

"Ah. I'm glad that place won't go to rack and ruin. My name's Albert Brownlee, and once you cross the stream you're on my land."

"Oh," said Alice.

"But you're welcome. Any time. So long's you ain't got a dog with you."

"We don't have a dog."

"You sisters?"

"No. This is my friend Anne. I'm Alice Mason."

"Pleased to meet you." The polar bear shook paws with Anne then Alice. "Where you off to then? Doing a bit of exploring? What's the saw for?"

"We're looking for a Christmas tree," said Alice politely. "Daddy said there was a farm here and we should ask and say we'll pay up to five pounds. No more, because we're using our own labour."

"Ah."

"Are those your trees?"

"They are."

"May we have one?"

"Five pounds?"

"No more," said Alice firmly. "Dad says if you could send the bill –"

"You sure you ain't got a dog?"

"Of course."

"Back at the castle?"

"No."

"Something bothering my sheep."

"We don't have a dog."

"Hm."

Alice glanced at Anne and the elfin mouth hid a smile.

"Follow me."

The polar bear ambled the way he had come, over the stream's wooden bridge, past the field. "This is called Bottom Field," it said, "and that there up the slope is Castle Field cos it meets your ground at the stream."

"You mean all that land with the bowing-down trees is ours?"

"It is. Too bad there ain't no firs'n'you wouldn't need to come poaching mine."

"We have asked."

"Mm."

They walked into the trees and the farmer – or polar bear – pointed. "You can have that one."

Alice followed the pointing finger.

"It's rather small," she said.

"What height's your ceilings?"

"I'm not sure."

"That tree's ten feet, an' as I recall – though I ain't been in the castle for years – there ain't no ceiling higher."

"It's too spindly," said Alice. "Look. There's a nice fat one, and it's not any taller. May we have that?"

The farmer looked at them, his red face serious. "It'll cost you."

Alice waited.

"You sure you ain't got a dog?"

Alice tightened her mouth making her cheeks stick out.

"Cost you an 'ome-made apple pie. That's my price, and I won't back down. Take it or leave it."

"We'll take it! Thank you! Thank you very much!"

Alice untied the saw and approached the tree. She couldn't reach the trunk for the heavy skirt of branches.

"It's awfully big when you're close to it," she whispered to Anne.

"And it's prickly."

They walked round it. Anne knocked snow off, as high as she could reach, but that didn't help.

"Got a problem have you?"

Alice shrugged.

"Here," said the farmer. He took the saw and stepped among the branches. He cut them one by one until the trunk was bare to knee-height. "Stand back." The saw bit bark, ripping quickly into the living wood, moisture on the blade, a large hand pressing the tree to keep the cut open, rip-rip, "There!" and the tree leaned, like a lady in green, fainting; a creak as the last fibres of the trunk tore, then crash! and a sparking of snow from the branches.

"Get your rope under it, then."

So they bound the tree until its arms were tight and the three of them swung one end onto the sledge, lifted the other end and tied it down.

"Wow!" said Alice. "Thank you very much!"

"Neighbours," said the farmer. "You sure you ain't got a dog?" he asked as they moved away. "With big feet. Half scared my sheep to death."

"No," called Alice. "Thank you."

"Don't forget my apple pie."

They rushed with many a Mush! Mush! across the tundra between the sea and Bottom Field. They bumped hollowly over the bridge. "Whoa!" cried Alice.

"What is it?" panted the other husky.

101

"We must build a cairn."

"What for?"

"That's what you do when you reach the North Pole."

"We should put up a flag."

"We haven't got a flag," said Alice.

So they built the cairn, not with stones, but from snowballs rolled around the white ground, leaving strange tracks as the snowballs grew. The cairn rose, tall as the children, taller once its head was on, rather grim as eyes were prodded in with a finger.

"He needs a smile," said Anne. "After all, it is Christmas."

"Three and a quarter days."

"It's getting a bit dark."

"We've spent ages building the snowman."

"We'll get pebbles on the beach."

They climbed down beside the stream through dry green grass in the snow, onto rocks.

"Watch you don't slip," warned Alice.

Water lapped curiously, licking boulders that might be good to eat. It trickled around the children, rustling seaweed.

"It's not really very nice," said Anne.

"It will be," said Alice. "In the summer. It might be safe for swimming. Imagine! Our very own patch of sea!"

"There's another polar bear."

"Where?"

"Or a sea-lion. Behind these rocks."

"I don't see anything." Alice stood tall on a boulder. "There's nothing. Let's get the pebbles and give the cairn his smile."

They lifted pebbles and hurried up through the dry grass and jammed the smile onto the snowman's face. "There you are Mr Cairn," said Anne. "I hope you are feeling better."

"I still don't see anything," said Alice, searching the rocks with a telescope made of her hands.

"It's getting quite dusky," said Anne.

"We didn't eat our emergency rations." Alice pointed her telescope back towards the forest where their tree had grown. She gazed at the farm. "Lights on in the farmhouse. That's the polar bear just going in. He seems in an awful hurry. He must have been somewhere else."

She faced the nearby trees. The telescope turned into hands as she rubbed heat into them. "It does look creepy," she said.

"We could save the emergency rations for supper," said Anne, staring around.

"Yes," agreed Alice. "It's only forty miles to home. Even hauling the tree it'll just take ten minutes. If we mush. Yes, let's go."

They strained on the rope to make the sledge move, then it jerked, and slipped along nicely; two heads down, then one glancing back, and another glancing back, making sure all was well.

Behind them the lights gleamed in the farmhouse, and the forest was almost black, and down on the beach the water whispered invisibly, while rocks shivered under tattered white bed sheets.

"I think I saw your sea-lion," said Alice. "Don't stop! We may not get the sledge moving again on this rough ground."

So they pulled. Lights ahead in the castle. The air thick with real dusk. Then shrubs blocked their view of the beach.

They pulled very hard then, and the sledge fizzed along, and heads turned towards the towering bowing trees, but mostly towards the beach with its whispering voices and the sense of something moving.

"There *is* something there!" cried Anne.

"Don't worry," panted Alice. "Just mush!"

"Mush!" said Anne, and they fairly trotted, towards the dark bulk of the castle, the sledge hissing, the tree bouncing, the saw, tied among the branches, vibrating miserably. Dusk drained almost to darkness making Anne's face a flash as she glanced back, while Alice stared ahead guiding them past the worst bumps, determined to be fearless.

They swirled through the orchard, swerved around the corner of the castle, the sledge scraping on one runner deep through to the gravel, then dropping, thank goodness! dropping and hissing swiftly, following the children as Alice led in a wide curve to take them through the archway safely.

"Shut the door!" she gasped, and they let the sledge slide as they darted back to the door; arms on fire with so much pulling, BANG! said the door solemnly, and its voice boomed under the arch.

"It can come through the gap in the wall," panted Anne.

"If there is anything," said Alice. "Leave the sledge. Let's get in."

TWENTY-ONE

Father was sitting, his heels on the Aga, reading a book, murdering a sandwich.

"Food!" cried Alice.

"Did you get a tree?"

"Yes," said Alice. "It'll cost us an apple pie. Our rations are all squashed. What are you eating, Richard? Will you be fit for dinner?"

"Ham and tomato."

"An 'ome-made apple pie," said Anne and went close to Father for a hug.

"Very good," said Father. "Who do we pay it to?"

"A polar bear called Albert Brownlee," said Alice. "He has the farm." Anne helped with the sandwich spreading. "D'you know, Richard, that all these trees are ours? Right to the stream? Then it's Castle Field and Bottom Field. Bottom Field goes down almost to the beach –"

"There was something on the beach," said Anne.

"Oh? What sort of thing?" Father put his book down.

Alice hacked through a tomato and turned to a cupboard for salt.

"What sort of thing?"

"It was *that* thing," whispered Anne. Alice looked at her.

Anne glanced back fearfully, then went to Father again. He put his arm round her, his lean face serious.

"Are you sure?"

"No," said Alice, "we are not sure. It was a feeling –"

"You said you saw it!" cried Anne.

"I only thought –"

"We ran home!"

"It was creepy," said Alice.

"It was that thing. It's come out of the sea."

Alice made the sandwiches. She placed them on the table, then found two Cokes in the fridge. She really hadn't seen anything. Perhaps a rook, or a gull feeding among the rocks. Certainly no tick-tack of claws, and certainly not that silly coat! Hadn't she stuffed it under the sea? Dropped boulders on it?

Or near it.

"It got into your head," said Anne, and Alice stared at her.

"It got into your head so much that you saw my giraffe-postcard as a leopard."

"I drowned it," whispered Alice. She couldn't swallow the sandwich. She couldn't help seeing Mum and Dad sprawled in their bedroom –

She felt her cheeks pull down, quivering. She didn't want to know about astral bodies!

Tears warmed her eyes, spilling onto her hands.

Daddy was beside her.

She sobbed in the safety of his arms. Even as she wept, she wondered where all the tears were coming from, for she really had been without fear. But if the thing was back, she would have to be fearless again. Fear could open the gates.

She sat up, independent, washed her face at the sink, ate her sandwich, drank her Coke.

"Where's Mum?"

"Took the car into town. There's always something else to buy at Christmas. She shouldn't be long."

"We shut the big door," said Alice.

"It's dark," said Anne.

"I'll put the outside light on," smiled Father.

"Is there one?"

"There's more than one. If you're finished grubbing I'll show you. Only found out what the switches were for today."

"Wait a minute." Alice left the kitchen. She went to her parents' bedroom. She found what she wanted immediately. The three linen bags lay on the mantelpiece, their raffia – broken when Mother wore the coat – was neatly knotted, as if Dad had known they might be needed. She ran to the kitchen, gave one to her father and one to Anne. Without a word they put them on. Alice had never removed hers. She put the third bag in her pocket for Mother.

"Ready," said Alice.

In the hall, Father showed them switches. "The end switch is for the light outside above the great door." He switched on, and a glow shone beyond the stained glass coats-of-arms. "And this one is for under the archway – *inside* the great door in other words." He opened the outside door and drew in his breath at the cold. An iron lamp beamed dimly onto the tree on the sledge. The foxface knocker winked at Alice. "And there are

107

three switches for the attics. I think."

"The Christmas tree's covered in snow," said Alice.

"Let's get it in," said Father.

So they dressed for Arctic weather, and hauled the tree under the archway, freed its arms from the rope, brushed off snow and squeezed it into the castle, Father wishing with a groan that they had kept it tied until it was through the doorways and along the wood-panelled passage. Anyway, into the long room it went, then it was laid on newspapers left over from unpacking to soak up drips.

"I want to walk up to the road," said Father. "See if Mum's coming."

"Walk?" said Anne. "Outside?"

Father jiggled his little bag of herbs.

"It'll be all right!" cried Alice. "Come on, Anne. Let's open the main door so Mum can drive straight in!"

They pushed the door, its iron studs digging into their palms. Snowflakes rushed through the lamplight. They used their booted feet to drag snow from the rail, and pulled the door wide.

Then they took a fatherly elbow each and trudged among the trees, giant feathers tumbling about them.

"Well." Father's torch beamed out. "A white Christmas for once."

Alice, holding Father's arm, looked back. The light above the gate shone clearly, though scored across by the tumbling weather. Lights in the windows were less bright. She searched for Melanie's cottage but saw only darkness and millionic movement. She wondered if anything else stirred in this silent world. She wondered if the tick-tack walked, muffled by the white ground.

They stopped where the lane met the road.

"Can you make out anything at all?" asked Father.

"I can see the light over the door," said Anne.

"I hear a car," said Alice, and they listened.

"Driving in low gear," said Father. "Quite right."

The noise growled louder. Lights too high for a car came glaring at them, roaring and swinging past, becoming a glow mingled with red tail lights, then fading.

They sighed.

"At least there's something moving. She could follow the tracks of that lorry . . ." Father was talking to himself.

"She isn't late?" asked Alice.

"Oh, no. But this . . ." Father's torch showed snow thickening on the road.

They stood close, three people huddled against winter, waiting for Mother, Alice trying not to worry, and trying not to feel that something awful could come crawling behind her.

"We can't stay here for long," said Alice.

"She might miss the turn-off," said Father.

"She might try to phone."

"You two go back."

"Alone?" whispered Anne.

Father didn't answer. The girls waited. Snow rushed down. Alice pulled her woolly hat over her ears but she couldn't hear the silence and eased it up again.

"We'll go back!" she decided suddenly.

"What!" said Anne.

"Well . . ." said Father, stomping to keep warm, glancing at Alice, then peering through the rushing dark. "I'll have to keep the torch to signal Mum. Are you sure . . .?"

"We can see the castle lights," said Alice boldly. "It's not completely dark. Come on Midget." She took Anne's hand and led her away from Father.

"I'd rather stay here," said Anne.

"I'm not letting that thing spoil our Christmas!" said Alice. "We've the tree to decorate and streamers to put up –" She made Anne walk with her. "– a table to polish for the long room –" They high-stepped through the snow. "– and I want to show Mum the stir-fry with prawns that Miss Marshall taught us. And we'll have to make Christmas cards . . ." she talked on. The castle lights shone brighter. The trees rustled suddenly all around, and snowflakes swirled. Anne clung against Alice.

"I don't like it."

"It's only the wind. You know – warm air rising, cooler air flowing in –"

"There's no warm air."

Anne stopped. They listened. The trees whispered, and Alice imagined the soft pummelling of waves on the beach.

"I can see your dad's torch."

"Keep going."

They stepped high. Snowflakes spun in a mad

dance and the trees sang from hollow throats. The wind pressed Alice's jacket against her back. Anne cried out.

"It's only the wind!" said Alice firmly, and they ran, deep snow clutching their feet, Alice's hair, below her hat, flying against her cheeks, Anne's arm tight. Then the rushing feathers flurried, letting her see the great door open under the light. Then the wind's soft hands pushed suddenly and Anne slipped, falling, but Alice jerked her up, and the trees howled, rattling branches, dropping snow into the darkness.

Alice – watching the door – sensed movement.

She turned her head. From among the trees a shadow slithered.

A chill that had little to do with the wind, slid down the skin of her spine. She stopped, crushing Anne's arm. Anne's face, pale in the darkness, peered up at her, then vanished as she too stared towards the trees.

"What?" whispered Anne into the wind.

Alice crouched, taking Anne down with her, making them small.

"There!" whispered Alice.

Something moved in the gloom of the snow. Something crept, softly dark, and branches rattled nervously. Anne's fingers bit Alice's arm –

"Don't move!" breathed Alice.

They watched, still as stones, as the crawling darkness broke from the trees and drifted it seemed – so vague was it – like smoke, but smoke with a purpose, pacing over the open ground, hesitating as a light blinked on in Melanie's cottage, crawling

again, sly, insubstantial as a dream, but so purpo-
seful, so determined, stalking towards the light in
the archway . . .

"It's going into the castle!" gasped Alice. "I
won't have it!" she whispered. Her arms quivered
and she felt her mouth twist with rage. "*I won't
have it!*" Energy burned within her. Tears of fury
mingled with snowflakes in her lashes.

"Keep down!" shrieked Anne in a whisper, but
the energy exploded through Alice, and she rose,
stretching her arms towards the sky, squeezing her
eyes shut to clear the tears –

"It's coming!" screamed Anne. "It's coming!"
But Alice's rage boiled in her throat and she
howled a sound that stunned the murmuring trees,
and though her ears heard Father's voice, she
didn't stop, but ran, stumbling to rescue her castle,
and the silent horror which was her enemy, sped
swiftly to meet her.

TWENTY-TWO

Alice had no idea what she meant to do. Even when the thing wheeled to face her, even when it closed on her, her rage took her forward, demanding contact, as if she could embrace that speeding darkness, and with the energy that scalded her mind, shrivel it into nothing.

She heard Daddy shouting.

She heard Anne screaming.

Her own voice filled her ears.

Light flickered behind her, but she ignored it, not understanding. She raged on.

The thing rose, the light bursting around it.

She lunged, clawing, shredding the air, as white brilliance blazed in the darkness.

She was fighting nothing.

She realized she was kneeling in the snow and that she was fearless.

Suddenly Mother was lifting her, and Dad, and little Anne embracing her. The light was the car headlights.

"I'm all right!" shouted Alice, anger still surging. "I'm all right!" And she marched triumphantly. She turned on Father. "We fought it off!" She turned on Mother. "We fought it off!"

She stood trembling. Father held her.

"Fought what off?" asked Mother feebly. "I only saw . . ."

"Let me go, Dad." Alice took the linen bag from her pocket and hung it around Mother's neck.

113

"That thing's back, Meg," said Father. "You three go inside. I'll put the car away." The car's windscreen wipers *whumped*. Father hesitated. He stared into Alice's face. "Well done," he said.

Alice dug through one of Mother's vegetable experiments. She let Father talk. Her mind held no thoughts; just the flavours of pastry and greens between her teeth so neat.

She helped wash up, laughing with Anne, glad Mother was home, but stunned by her experience. Then a row of coloured lights clicked on, and her mind and brain came together, and she was fully alive, finding herself in the long room, with Father kneeling at an electric socket, having switched on the fairy lights which curved across the floor.

"They still work," said Alice.

"You've come back to us," smiled Daddy.

"Where's Anne?" She remembered Anne had needed a lot of comforting too.

"Helping Mum. Putting shopping in cupboards. Right. Let's get this tree up." Daddy stared at the tree and the tea chest which was to be the tree's container. "We need something to weigh the box down – I know –" He grabbed Alice, and with enormous grunts strained to lift her.

"Help! Help!"

Father dropped her on her feet. "No. We'd need a crane."

"Beast. Face it, Dad, we'll have to go outside for stones."

"Outside?" Father sat on the edge of the tea chest.

"Scared, Dad?" asked Alice.

"You know," said Father, as if he hadn't heard, "I was always told that real bravery was doing something you're afraid to do, but . . ."

He held his hand out to Alice, and she touched it, then went and sat in the inglenook. The fire breathed hot on her face.

"You," said Father, and Alice saw he was thinking something out as he spoke. "If you had run at that thing *feebly*, you know, *uncertainly* – I think it would have been the finish of you. It was your boldness – not, covering up fear – not, going ahead despite fear – but doing the job with no fear at all. I don't quite see why, but it was *that* which made things happen as they did."

Daddy eased himself off the tea chest and sat in an armchair, leaning towards the fire. "As if your fearlessness made the wheels of the universe turn." He used his fingers like cogs on wheels. "As if your fearlessness made circumstances work for you – Mum arriving with the car at the right second . . ." He paused.

"It's not the chaps who go into battle scared, who come out better men – it's those who go in better men – they come out better than before." Firelight glowed on his skin. "I've never seen anything so brave."

He smiled.

There was a moment of harmony, then Father stood up, and they went to the kitchen. They chatted with the slaves packing the cupboards, then stepped into their wellingtons and almost immediately found stones sheltering near the dustbins.

115

Then up went the tree, its stump in a basin of water – "So it doesn't get dry and drop needles," said Father – inside the tea chest, then stones were packed, also inside the tea chest, to grip the trunk and balance their new guest in her heavy green dress.

Father draped the lights around the tree, switching them on, and Alice fetched Anne. They hung worms of shimmering foil, silver, blue and crimson among the branches, and stood back, frowning, then Anne suggested arranging big loops near the bottom of the tree and smaller ones towards the top. They did this, up and down the step-ladder a hundred times, then with very little rearranging, it looked just about as grand as it could.

Next, baubles and glass balls were suspended in exactly the right places, and the gold star that had gazed down from the top of every Christmas tree that Alice could remember, was put up by Father (because Alice couldn't reach, even with the steps) and they all agreed that with coloured paper around the tea chest it would be the best Christmas tree in the world.

"And if we can keep that thing outside . . ." said Alice.

"I had a word with Melanie on the phone," said Father.

"What if it comes down the wide chimney?"

"I hammered wedges up." Father's hand rested on Alice's shoulders. "The other chimneys aren't big enough. I checked every single one. I'm looking after you, you know."

"It was like a great ghost," whispered Alice,

remembering the shadow speeding across the snow. "I thought it would be a leopard. I think the coat was in the midst of it –"

"Don't talk about it," said Anne.

"The coat definitely doesn't turn into a leopard," said Father gently, "because it's made of the skins of several leopard cubs. It never was one leopard. Perhaps, though, it's an *idea* of a leopard. . . Let's sit at the fire. I'll make some tea in a minute." He sat back in the armchair.

"We'll sort it out," he assured them. "Melanie's preparing herself. Whatever that means."

A log settled, spinning sparks onto the hearth.

The Christmas tree blinked on and off.

Anne sighed, then grinned secretly at Alice.

Alice knew that despite their strange adventure her little friend was happier than she had ever been.

Headlights swept the outside of the windows. A blue flash swung across the glass.

Anne leapt up and looked out.

"It's the police," she said.

TWENTY-THREE

Father looked at Alice. Alice raised her eyebrows.

"I'll go," sighed Father.

Alice knelt on the window seat beside Anne. A policeman and someone else stepped from a Range Rover.

"It's the polar bear," said Alice.

"The tree's ours now," said Anne.

They sat together, waiting curiously as voices came through the hall.

"Alice and Anne," said Father. "This is Sergeant Peckham. And Mr Brownlee."

"Hello," said Alice.

"Hello," said Anne.

"You'd better meet my wife," said Father. "Sit down. Alice, ask Mum to come through. We were thinking about a pot of tea . . .? Ask her to make some tea . . ."

Alice and Anne rushed to find Mother, and returned with tea and biscuits, and a lot of impatience.

". . . introduce myself to newcomers –" The policeman and Mr Brownlee, stood up as Mother came in and they were introduced.

"Routine," said Father smiling at Mother.

"It's a terrible night for a routine visit," said Mother. She stared at the farmer.

"Well now, Mrs Mason," replied the policeman, "it is and it isn't. Home-made bisuits? Well now. What I mean is, that, as I was saying to your husband, Mr Mason here –"

Alice tightened her face round a giggle and glanced at Anne who nudged her.

"I like to introduce myself to newcomers, so you know who to come to for help, and so's I know who might need help. Though you got good neighbours with Jack and Melanie. Pretty girl, though some say . . . Well." A look from the farmer. "Albert says he asked the children about your dog –"

"We haven't got a dog," said Mother.

"Didn't you believe us!" said Alice, suddenly angry.

"Alice!"

"We told you at least ten times!"

The policeman took charge. "Albert didn't mean that, Miss, but you got to understand that livestock is important, and when animals are killed everything has to be double checked –"

"Killed?" said Father.

"Killed, sir. That's why this is more than a routine visit. You haven't got a dog. Right. Any other pets?"

Father shook his head.

"In a place this size," said Sergeant Peckham, "you could easily keep a . . . panther, or a leopard."

"What would anyone want with a panther or a leopard!" said Father.

"You haven't got one?"

"No. Nor an elephant, nor a rhinoceros –"

"Dick," said Mother.

Alice thought she saw a smile struggle on the

farmer's red face. He said, "I don't suppose George could spell 'rhinoceros'."

"And Albert," said the policeman to Alice, after a moment's thought, "doesn't believe anything, unless he's weighed it, cut it up and made a profit on it." And he nodded heavily, obviously well-pleased at having evened the score between himself and Albert, and at the same time taken the sting out of Alice's indignation.

Father grinned, then looked serious. "You said animals were killed."

"Strictly speaking, sir," said George, "died. Not killed. Not savaged or nothing. Albert found 'em just after he met the girls. Three sheep with their legs at all angles and some sort o' prints in the snow, but not clear what with early dusk and snow still coming down."

"Sounds as if they died of fright," said Father politely.

"Maybe. Albert called the vet straight off. We'll know in a day or two."

Father made more polite enquiries as the sergeant finished his tea. Then, "We'll be off, Mr Mason." The policeman's eyebrows sent everyone's attention to the biscuit plate. "You'll be an asset, Mrs Mason, at the church bazaar. Not that there ain't plenty of ladies around here who bake, but there's home baking and home baking – if you know what I mean." He looked at Alice and Anne. "And if you don't mind a bit of advice, young ladies, don't stray too far from home until we catch that animal."

He moved to the door, taking Albert reluctantly

from the biscuit plate. "I'm having the safari parks checked," said Sergeant Peckham, "but if you could keep your eyes open . . ."

They faded into the hall.

"Oh!" gasped Anne. "I thought he was going to ask if we'd seen anything! What would your dad have said?"

"Well, he didn't ask," said Alice. "And I don't want to think about it –"

"They liked my biscuits!" said Mother triumphantly as she cleared away the cups.

"You *must* think about it," said Anne so quietly that Alice looked at her. "Let's sit at the fire."

"What?" said Alice as they huddled into the inglenook. She really did not want to think about the coat. She felt safe in the castle now. Outside was different, but there was no need to go out. At least, not beyond the woodpile, or the coal store.

"Don't you see?" said Anne, and her old-lady curls bobbed at her cheeks. "It's attacking other creatures . . ."

"It frightened them."

"It stole their astral energy. Remember your mum and dad, how they were sprawled about?"

"Dad was curled up," whispered Alice.

"It might go into the village . . ."

Alice started.

"It might kill someone," said Anne. Her mouth made a smile but her eyes were cool like shadows on snow.

"What can we do?" croaked Alice.

"Talk to Melanie."

Something clicked in Alice's brain. She saw

Dad's fingers pretending to be wheels of the universe. She saw the car lights blazing and the creature vanishing. If the car's arrival was a wheel meshing perfectly, perhaps Melanie was another — perhaps buying the castle even, was a turn of a universal cog, to put them, and the coat into a place where things could be worked out.

"Yes," she said, as Father returned from seeing Mr Brownlee and the police sergeant out, "we must see Melanie."

TWENTY-FOUR

They woke to the brilliance of snow and sunshine.

They breakfasted, full of chatter as Father phoned his office. "They'll call if there are any problems," he said. "Aha! Real eggs! I can smell the straw. What's the plan for today, you two?"

"Holly-hunting," said Alice firmly.

"Outside," said Anne. "We thought we'd visit Melanie."

"Good idea. I couldn't get much sense out of her when I phoned. We should ask them over. Meg?"

"There's so much to do," said Mother.

"What about Christmas Day?" said Alice.

"Well," said Father, "people often like to stay at home at Christmas."

"Leave it just now," said Mother. "Once we get organized . . ."

"You'll tell her about yesterday. When I spoke to her she seemed in a daze." Father stared at Alice seriously. "I suppose," he said, "we are depending on her to sort this out. It's hardly a job for the police." He went on staring at Alice. "Off you go then."

"Right."

"Go on."

"Right. Right, Anne. Wellies. Let's go."

"Bye, darlings," said Mother vaguely, and Anne grinned at Alice, delighted to be a darling.

"We may as well take the sledge," said Alice, so

they trailed over the snow, snug in anoraks and woolly hats, Alice with the Stanley knife, a cork on its blade, in her pocket, Anne with bin-bags for the holly.

They left the sledge at the cottage gate, and Melanie welcomed them. "I was just going to feed the chickens," she said, leading them to the kitchen. "Then I've got a batch of baking to do for Christmas. Sit down. I'll put the kettle on. It's some time since I had breakfast. Don't you want anything then?"

She looked at the girls, put the kettle down with a clang, and sat facing them, her beautiful eyes solemn behind her glasses.

"So," she said quietly. "It isn't over. I wasn't sure. Last night – in the evening – I had a bad feeling –"

"It's a wonder you didn't hear me screaming."

"Couldn't hear nothing above that wind. I went into the front parlour to see if anything was going on outside, then I saw the car, and you all there . . . I wasn't needed just then, but . . ." She gazed at Alice. "It was you. I've been preparing. Just in case. But it was you. Now I can feel it . . ."

"What?"

"Well, I usually know when something's wrong, and when this bad feeling came over me – I don't know – something held me back. As I say, as if I wasn't needed – that someone else just as strong was doing it for me."

"Doing what? D'you mean me?"

"I mean you. Providing the power to send that thing off with its tail between its legs!"

"But what power? I don't have –"

"Yes, you do. Oh, my dear, yes you do! You got power the like I haven't seen –"

"But what is it! Where does it come from?"

"Why, it comes from inside." She smiled mysteriously. "Which is outside." She laughed. "Don't expect to understand, my dears. There are a thousand things I could say that you couldn't grasp. And no use asking your dad or mum. No, nor anyone else. You either have eyes to see – or you don't. It's as simple as that." She focused her gaze full on Alice, and Alice sat, her breath warm on her lips, ever-so-slightly afraid of this young woman.

"Perhaps," said Melanie quietly, "one day you really will understand. If you do, it will come from within, not through someone else."

"It killed sheep," said Anne suddenly.

"What?"

"Albert Brownlee," said Alice. "We met him yesterday and he wouldn't believe we didn't have a dog. After we got home he came with Sergeant Peckham to tell us something had killed three of his sheep. He still thought we had a dog. There were no marks on the sheep, so we thought –"

Melanie turned her head sharply towards the back door.

"The chickens!" she whispered. "I thought they were quiet!"

"Oh!" cried Alice.

Melanie ran.

"Come on!" said Alice.

125

Beyond the garden, the sea lay heavy on the shore.

Melanie's footprints broke a path in the snow.

"She's just standing," said Anne.

Melanie was gazing into an enclosure made of wire mesh.

"She's crying," said Alice. They approached. Within the enclosure, nothing moved. Lumps beneath the snow caused Alice to grip Anne's arm.

A rook cawed high in the trees.

On the beach, a few yards away, water rippled and sighed.

Melanie tugged a wooden peg that held the door shut. She went into the enclosure and crouched by one of the mounds, stroking away snow. Tan feathers appeared. She looked back at Alice and Anne.

"You go off now," she said quietly.

"Are you sure?" said Alice. "We could help –"

"No. Thank you, Alice. But I got things to do." Her hair flashed in the cold sunlight as she looked towards the chicken coop. "I got things to do," she whispered. She stood up, and something in her manner alarmed Alice. "I got preparations to make. Real serious preparations. This is a terrible thing. It's time it was ended. You can do one thing for me . . ."

"Yes?"

"Phone my Jack. Tell him to come home straight away. Dial eight-four and let it ring. The phone's in the hall. Do you know how to pray? No matter. A child's prayer is best. You must both of you pray that I have strength. Just that."

Alice and Anne glanced at each other.
"Don't wait till night time," said Melanie. "Start the prayer and let it continue in your heart whatever you're doing. It's more important than you know." She stepped closer staring at them through the mesh. "It opens another sort of gate," she said.

Alice put the phone down. "He's coming," she told Anne. They closed the front door of the cottage and trudged to the sledge.
"It's hateful!" said Anne. "That beastly thing should go back where it came from!"
"Don't worry," said Alice. "Take the reins, Husky! Mush! Mush!"
Slowly at first, the smaller husky leaned on the reins, then as the sledge slid forward, her anxious glance brightened, and they trotted, huskies in wellingtons, past the castle, up the lane between the bowing trees. "Caw!" shouted Alice, and a rook rose, circling high in the winter sunlight, flapping blackly onto a branch.
Across the thick white road they went, parking the sledge at the roadside. "There's been nothing along here for hours!" cried Alice. They stared critically at a holly tree and made thoughtful faces, and the more they thought, the more thoughtful their faces became, with brows glowering and mouths dragged sideways into cheeks, until they shrieked, sending laughter along the empty road-way, dashing their pure voices against the winter trees, setting the rook hunching and stretching on its high branch.

"There's not a single berry," moaned Alice.

"There must be another tree!" cried Anne. They looked. The ground at this side of the lane rose, carrying the trees higher and higher away from the children, showing them roots like giant fingers gripping the ground.

"There's not so much snow in there," commented Alice. "And it's very rough. We'll leave the sledge here."

"Do you see a holly tree?"

"We won't go far."

Alice led Anne among the trunks. Almost at once they stopped and looked back at the road and the little sledge, already lonely.

Alice moved on, pushing aside twiggy branches, watching snow slip from the green body of a fir tree, feeling ice crack under her wellingtons, breathing the smell of earth and sweet decay.

"There's one!"

They crashed forward.

Out came the knife, off came its cork, rustling open went the black bin-bag, its mouth gaping between Anne's tiny hands, then *slice!* went the knife and holly dropped, like fish into a seal, into the bag, and Anne said, "There's a lovely bunch of berries," and Stanley bit.

Many an "Aow!" followed an "Ouch!" as the holly defended itself, but the bag filled and was shaken making green spikes slit through the plastic and stare out at freedom.

"Shake it down more!" said Alice. "We can cut lots, yet."

"The bag's splitting all over. I'll tie a knot at the

128

top." Anne took the bag's ears and knotted its mouth shut. "Do you think we should pray?"

Alice opened another bag. "Now?"

"Melanie said it was important."

"We can't kneel down here."

"People at funerals don't kneel."

"I don't suppose God will mind," said Alice. "Should we?"

"There's nobody to see. Melanie said—"

"All right. What shall we say?"

Anne said, "Close your eyes. Concentrate."

Alice closed her eyes, putting darkness between herself and the trees. She smelt the holly leaves. She heard snow slipping from branches and thudding on the ground. She giggled.

"Stop it!" said Anne. "You're making me laugh. We've got to try."

Silence again.

"It's hard keeping your balance," said Alice.

"Maybe that's why people kneel down."

"We're not doing very well. You say some words."

A deep breath from Anne. The silence of the trees seemed to drop around the children. Alice felt a shiver cross her back. She saw light behind her eyelids but knew it was a light inside her head. The shiver spread, chilling the backs of her arms –

"Help Melanie," whispered Anne, and the rook cawed. "Help her to be strong. Please help her to be very strong and kill that monster. Please send it away. Please help us."

Alice heard herself breathing. The bin-bag rustled. She felt a smile shaping her mouth, a smile that billowed from deep inside. On the slope above, a branch rustled.

She opened her eyes.

Anne opened her eyes wide.

Branches rustled louder.

Alice stared.

"What is it?" gasped Anne.

Alice pushed the blade of her knife deliberately into the cork. She placed the knife in her pocket and lifted the bag.

"Let's go," she said.

Crash!

"It's that thing!" screamed Anne.

They began to run.

TWENTY-FIVE

They ran down the slope among the trees, booted feet beating the earth, stamping the snow, faces dodging branches, the bin-bag bouncing, tight in Alice's fist. It ripped, shredding into black ribbons, spilling holly on the white ground, Anne leaping desperately onto the road, Alice behind her, "Leave the sledge!" But Anne was racing, snow flying from her heels, between the bowing trees –

Alice fell, rolling the last yard onto the road. "Oh!" Her breath bumped out of her. Up the slope the trees cried *crash!* as their branches sprang together and heavy feet came thumping and slipping.

Heavy feet!

Alice let her woolly-capped head relax onto the road. Boots approached over the tree roots. Boots built for pushing a spade into the earth. Grave-digger's boots, thought Alice.

"Anne!" she shouted. She sat up. Anne was almost at the castle. "Anne!" She smiled, and stood up as Jack came down the slope.

"Hello!" said Jack. "Are you all right?" he asked, seeing Alice brushing snow from her clothes.

"Yes, thank you."

"I've got to get home." He nodded up the slope. "Shortcut," he said. "Thanks for phonin', by the way. See you later. Here's your little sister."

Alice smiled, but didn't correct him. Then Anne

approached, glancing shyly at Jack as he passed.

"He told me my little sister was coming," said Alice.

"He knows I'm not," said Anne. "I didn't see you fall. I didn't mean to leave you."

"It doesn't matter. We'll have to start again with the holly."

It was lunch time when they left one very bare holly tree. Anne had said they shouldn't cut so much foliage, but Alice asked how far from home she wanted to go to find another, so they had sliced ruthlessly until their hands could suffer no more jags.

Then with bin-bags slit and bursting on the sledge, they went carefully along the lane and under the archway. They threw the bags into the hall and put the sledge in its stable. Their afternoon would be used decorating the castle.

"Somebody's in the coach house," said Anne.

"The pottery," said Alice, noticing snow scraped back by the door, and the loose padlock.

They went into the pottery, pulling the door shut. Melanie, wandering from shelves to table, paused, taller, thought Alice, more alive; as beautiful as a deer, as close to nature as a flowing stream. She smiled, Melanie, her blue eyes behind the glasses kind but distant, delighted-to-see-them, but three-quarters somewhere else.

Alice looked at Anne, and Anne looked up at Alice.

"Is it really her?" whispered Anne.

"Come in, my dears," breathed Melanie. "It's

132

really me. My astral can't do the work." She showed them the biscuit-coloured pepper pots in her hands. She put the pots on the table adding to the rows already waiting. Behind her the kiln clicked and buzzed, cooking pottery. A gas heater fizzed. She said nothing more, but wandered again from shelf to table.

She stood looking at the pots. Her eyes regarded a plastic bucket half-deep with thick pink liquid. Beside the bucket was a rubber ball with a spout, and a sponge just big enough to wash one finger at a time.

Melanie's lazy gaze crossed the children, and wandered to the kiln. She took from under the kiln an oblong shelf, heavy as stone, and put it on the table.

"Can we help?" asked Alice.

Melanie's hair sparkled under the strip lights. Her eyelids closed and opened slowly as she shook her head.

"Are you all right?"

Melanie's nod went up and down.

"I'm sorry about the chickens."

The eyelids closed and opened in agreement.

"She doesn't want to talk," said Anne, and Melanie smiled. She sat on a stool at the table, lifted a wooden spoon and stirred the thick liquid. She lifted a pepper pot, popped it head-first in for a drink, pulled it out, one *shake!* and stood it on the stone shelf.

"She's glazing them," said Anne.

"I know!" said Alice.

In went another pot, *shake!* and out.

133

"How does she manage not to smudge them!" whispered Anne, for Melanie held only the tiniest edge of a pot's bottom as she dipped, and by some swift miracle turned it right way up on the shelf without seeming to change her grip. Dip, went another. Then another. And when a row was complete, she stood up, leaning over the row, and using the rubber ball, squeezed another colour of glaze into flower shapes around the shoulders of each pot. Then she started the second row. Once, she stopped her rhythmic dipping and, mouth wide, wiped the base of a pot with the sponge.

"I shook a drip onto its bottom," she whispered, "and that would make it stick to the shelf."

The girls nodded.

"I'm sorry for being so quiet," said Melanie in a voice distant like the sea, "but there is a great battle ahead, and I am preparing. The work –" Her beautiful head tilted and her hands ceased dipping for a moment as she gestured at the table. "– the work occupies my brain. It fills the need to be busy in this world, but . . . my mind is elsewhere. It is a cleansing. A purification, my dears, for don't we get clogged with earthly things? The desperation of the Little Self for growth and recognition is like armour weighing us down. I am shedding that armour now. In a day or two . . ."

Her eyes closed and opened. "Though if something happens, I may have to face the coat before I am ready . . ." She seemed to have forgotten the two girls. They moved to the door.

"Your prayer helped."

They looked at her. Her hands moved in rhythm.

"There is no need to die. My chickens . . . are just chickens. Your prayer reminded me of that. They are little souls. It was simply their time to move on. If we truly realized the great secrets, we would rejoice at death when a soul has striven in life." She sat still, eyes closed, pepper pots in their pink robes standing in row. Row upon row.

Alice pushed the door.

"Never be complacent," breathed Melanie. "Those who are complacent experience real death." Her eyes shone, full on Alice, ablaze with a light that set Alice stepping back against the door. Anne's little fingers found Alice's palm.

"The complacent," whispered Melanie, "are already dead."

They stepped into the snow and shut the door.

"She scares me," said Anne.

"Yes."

"What did she mean?"

"I don't know."

Alice knew there were things to discuss. But not now. Perhaps in a week, or in a month, or in all the years ahead, she would sit with Melanie, trying to unravel her strange words.

"I'm hungry," said Anne.

"Yeh!" said Alice.

They invaded the kitchen.

TWENTY-SIX

A pot on the Aga pumped out stew smells. Soup erupted with volcanic slaps, and baking, in the ovens, Alice knew, was swelling to edible lightness, sweetening the air.

Mother sighed over the table, cutting pastry circles, prodding them into baking trays, turning them into mincemeat pies; not as happy as she should have been.

"Help yourselves to soup," said Mother. "There's cold meat for a sandwich."

"Where's Dad?" asked Alice. "Soup plates," she commanded, and Anne, who knew where everything was, brought them quickly.

"Repairing furniture, I think."

So they ate, then found Father in the hall, the guts of a dining chair around him, tools, and the fire fairly galloping up the chimney.

"What are you doing?" asked Anne.

"It's hard to say." Father beamed. "The upholstery is rotted and there's a hundred years of dust among the horsehair. Springs," he said, waving at large metal springs scattered on the floor. "Hope I can put 'em back. What are you up to? Did you tell Melanie? About yesterday?"

"It killed her chickens," said Alice.

"What?"

"Jack's with her. At least, he's home. Melanie's in the pottery. She's gone all weird. She asked us to pray for her." She turned to Anne. "We were

136

supposed to keep it going."

"Keep it going?" said Father.

"The prayer," said Alice. "We'd better do it again. She said it helped. Do you want to join in?"

"Well. . . Should I put on my best suit?"

"This is serious, Dad."

"*You* giggled," said Anne.

"Shut up, Midget, and say the words."

"How can I shut up and say the words?"

Alice smiled and they prayed again, Father cross-legged among tools, the children standing. Then Alice and Anne, with stepladders and Sellotape (for they were forbidden to use drawing pins on the precious woodwork) put up the holly.

They began high around the hall, quickly discovering they had to dust the panelling before the tape would stick. They worked artistically, turning each holly bunch this way and that. They draped streamers from corner to corner (sneaking in drawing pins after all, because the tape would not hold the weight), glad that Alice could reach, tiptoes on the top step then press the pins in place.

"There!" she said with satisfaction.

The fire flickered in silent applause.

"Pretty good!" said Anne.

Alice forgot her satisfaction. The smile remained on her face but slipped from her mind as something else pushed in.

"What are you thinking?" said Anne.

Alice stood, quite relaxed.

"Can you hear something?" asked Anne. "You look like Melanie looked, in the graveyard –"

Alice silenced her with a finger.

Then she knew.

"Melanie wants us," she said.

Anne blew a little laugh. "What?"

"She's still in the pottery. Come on." Alice grinned. "She wants us!"

They zoomed past Father, hopped into wellingtons and anoraks, approved of Mother's baking by stealing a mince pie each, and ran to the coach house.

On the table stood the pepper pots – now with their wives, the salt pots – enough to fill the kiln when the glaze dried.

And Melanie dreamier than ever, smiling, saying, "Thank you, Alice. Would you keep an eye on the kiln for me? Turn it to low in about an hour. Could you put the bungs in, here –" She held a ceramic plug showing how it fitted into a hole in the kiln door. "– and here, in the top. It will stay on all night, and my Jack will switch it off in the morning, but I'll need him with me this evening. If you wouldn't mind, my dears?"

"Of course not –"

"But how did you know –?" squeaked Anne.

"Ssh! Are you going now? Could we stay? I love pottery!"

"Make a pot?" murmured Melanie. "Why, yes. Let me see. Use this clay. And the wheel?"

"Yes, please!"

"Switch it on there. With dry hands, mind. I must go. Thank you for coming."

"Goodnight," said Alice.

"Goodnight," said Anne.

"Blessings," smiled Melanie. "Blessings."

They closed the door behind her.

"But how did you know!" cried Anne, tugging at Alice's arm. "She was expecting us!"

Alice shrugged, raising her eyebrows, a fat smile pushing at her cheeks. "Magic," she said.

"Come off it, Blobby!"

"I tell you it was magic! I just knew she wanted us."

"What did it feel like?"

"It didn't feel like anything. What does any idea feel like? Me first on the wheel!"

"Me first! Me first!"

And the sensible conversation exploded into a rough-and-tumble to get at the clay, then a truce when Alice found grey smears on her anorak.

"I've got an apron!" cried Anne. She threw off her outers and they howled at the apron trailing over her feet and the strings going round her almost three times.

"Hoist it up," ordered Alice, and they arranged a tuck in the middle to shorten it. "I can't find another. You start. Mum's got a plastic apron —"

"Don't leave me."

"It's not dark."

"You can borrow this. We can't both use the wheel at the same time."

"I'll be back in a minute!" said Alice.

She made a face, and went out heaving the door to shut it. Anne's fearfulness was sometimes annoying. Nothing could hurt her in the pottery. Jack had boarded up the skylight.

Dusk was settling on the courtyard. They had

139

spent longer than Alice realized, decorating the hall. She turned her head, deliberately not hurrying, defying fear. This half-dark did strange things to the crowded chimneys on the castle roof.

Alice glanced back at the snow-soft wall between the courtyard and the sea. She glimpsed the hothouse peeping coldly. From the pottery door, a crack of light spilled onto the snow.

She went into the kitchen.

Something was wrong.

TWENTY-SEVEN

Rounds of pastry for shortbread sat on the floury table, smelling of butter. Christmas pies in rows, reminded Alice of pepper pots. Heat blasted from the Aga.

Mother was gone.

"Mum," moved Alice's lips.

She hurried in the corridors, wellingtons whumping, "Mum," on her breath. She stopped at Mother's bedroom door. Horror at the memory of the last time – but the room was empty.

She began to run, "Mum!" through the long room, "Mum!" banging into the short passage with its linen-fold panels that had been there before any of the family was born, and would would be there after they were dead – into the hall –

Father, the chair looking like a chair again, instead of a gutted animal, relaxing with tea and a sandwich, and Mother, sitting up straight on a cushion on the hearth, enjoying the fire.

"Alice, what a noise."

"Everything all right?" said Father.

Alice stared. "Ye-es."

"What's wrong?" asked Father.

"I thought . . ." Alice shrugged. "It's nothing. Can I borrow an apron? Or an old shirt. We're potting."

"Did Melanie give you permission?" asked Mother.

141

"Of course! May I have a sandwich? Thanks!"

"That's my lunch!" cried Father. "Isn't it?" he asked, as Mother shook her head.

"You had soup," she reminded him, "and a slice of pie."

"Ah," said Father. "You may have the sandwich." Which was just as well, since the last bite was being pushed into Alice's mouth by Alice's dimpled fingers. She smiled, her cheeks fatter-than-ever with bread and cold ham. She mumbled, pointing at Father's mug.

Father gave her his you-must-be-joking look, but she wrestled the mug from him, trying not to laugh, not to explode her sandwich over him.

And as she sipped, something niggled.

Perhaps it was the deserted kitchen, with everything in the middle of being used; like the *Marie Celeste*.

But Mum was here.

"The apron," mumbled Alice.

"I need it in the kitchen," said Mother. "Ask Daddy for a shirt."

Father sighed.

"A shirt," said Alice. "I beg you. Beg. Beg."

"You'd better go with her, Dick, or she'll take your best one."

"I'm not stupid, Mother."

"Sometimes you are careless," said Mother waving a finger at the clay streaks on Alice's anorak.

"Follow me," groaned Father.

"Check the shortbread, will you, Dick?"

"Tramp, tramp," said Dick. "Into the most

142

magnificent room in the world. Isn't the tree excellent! When will you put up the holly in here? You made a good job of the hall."

"We're only potting for a little while. Then we've to shove the bungs in the kiln for Melanie. This evening, I suppose."

Niggle.

Alice followed Father, took his arm, down the corridor warm with wood, into the bedroom.

"One shirt," said Father, hauling a shirt from a drawer. "Has Anne something?"

"Melanie's apron."

Niggle.

"You've to check the shortbread," said Alice, frowning.

"Is something wrong?"

"I've got a feeling . . ."

"Anne?" said Father, moving to the door.

"No. The feeling came just as I left her. She was OK then."

They walked in corridors towards the kitchen.

Alice thought.

She had pulled a face at Anne. She had stepped outside, seeing the castle's crowded chimneys; the wall and hothouse, mysterious in the dusk; light from the coach house door lying bright on the snow.

The picture of light on the snow stayed with her.

She drew in a breath.

"What?" snapped Father.

"Oh!" gasped Alice. "Oh!" She began to run, desperately slowly it seemed –

"Alice!"

143

Something Watching

– through the kitchen with its warm smells –
"Alice?"
– into the courtyard –
"Alice!"
"Annie!" she screamed.
The coach house was dark.

TWENTY-EIGHT

She slipped as she reached it – that horrid gap, wide enough for a dog to step through. Father's hand caught her elbow and hoisted her. "Wait!" he whispered.

They waited, staring in.

Alice saw an eye, red and circular. Something burped and clicked. She realized it was the kiln and the eye was the kiln's eye – the vent in the door glowing red-hot. She couldn't see Anne. The table waited, vague in the darkness, with the glaze bucket towering over the pepper pots. The gas heater murmured. She wondered how she could see at all, and looked up.

"Dad!" She pointed at the ceiling. The strip lights were glowing, soft rods of luminance fighting unnatural shadows.

"They must still be switched on," whispered Father in awe.

"We've got to find Anne!" gasped Alice.

"You can't go in there!" snarled Father, hauling her away.

"I fought it off before!"

"It's stronger!" cried Father in a desperate whisper. "Its darkness has smothered the lights! Wait. We'll use the car again! Headlights! I'll need the keys!" he shrieked.

"*Call on it!*" whispered Alice. She clenched his arm with iron fingers. "Keep it at the door! *Beast!*" she screamed. "*Beast! Come and get us beast!*"

145

"What are you doing!"

"Calling it off Anne! You do it!" she yelled at
her father. "Keep it at this door!" He leaned on the
door, shutting it, and she ran; past the shirt on the
kitchen floor; past the sparkle of the Christmas
tree in the long room. Mother's voice by the hall
fire, jangled at her, but Alice struck the bunch of
light switches, clicking them on. Up the stairs she
raced, smashing aside the door to my lady's room
in the keep, then the door to the attic. Dad had
been right. The lights were on – far apart, but
sharp enough to show the ancient beams her feet
must tread, and tread swiftly. Rubber struck wood
as she ran, concentrating so as not to stumble
through the ceilings below, muscles hard in her
legs, ignoring the caverns of darkness that gaped
beside her. Floorboards beat beneath her feet and
she fairly flew. Annie! Let her be safe! God, let
Annie be safe! Melanie, help us! Help us!

The wall.

The wall with the door to the pottery store
room.

She leaned on the door, listening, panting.
Father's voice, faintly, and banging, like his fist on
the big door of the coach house. *Keep it busy!*

She found the door handle and pulled. She stared
between the shelves. It was very dark. "Annie!" she
whispered. She began to lift down pots from a
shelf, quietly.

"Anne!"

Light escaped from the attic into the store. She
saw a rectangle of light on the floor, but it was
merely a grid above the kiln to let heat up, catching

the glow from the strip lights. But it helped her see. "Anne!" she breathed. Dad's voice and thumping. Alice slid between the shelves. There was no movement, no sound in the store room. She made out the pots in rows, pots in endless clusters on soaring shelves. The rail around the top of the stair. The glisten of snow beneath the skylight, melting. Her glance went to the skylight. The dusk outside, lighter than in the room, was half filled with planks. Jack's work.

Downstairs, Father's voice, and tappings of his knuckles, and a *tick-tack* that froze Alice's spine. "Oh, Anne!" she whispered. "Where are you!"

Could she have got into the attic above the castle? Alice half turned, but knew it was impossible, for all the pots had been on the shelves, blocking the way. And the skylight was nailed shut, so she wasn't on the roof.

She moved. "Anne," she breathed.

She walked quietly, avoiding the grid on the floor, staring hard along the bottom shelves. Anne could have rolled underneath. She got close to the top of the stairs. The smothered glow of the strip lights reached up to her. She backed away. Beyond the rail, something shone dim in the darkness. Was it a pot? A paper bag. Anything at all worth her precious seconds!

She moved around the rail. She went close to the pale thing, bending down. Something leapt at her, silently, making her gasp, around her neck a grip of bone, against her cheek –

"Oh, God!" cried Alice. "Annie!"

*   *   *

147

"We've got to get out!" whispered Alice, but the grip around her neck was solid. She held her friend by the waist and took her, silently, oh, so silently! across the floor, past the warm grid. "You must let go!" urged Alice. "We must climb between the shelves!" She eased Anne's little fingers loose, and guided her, half lifted her, onto a shelf, and followed – what a noise their clothes made! What scuffing of boots on timber! Through she went, Anne, Alice rolling beside her into the attic, Anne's arms throttling her instantly as she closed the door. They turned, and beneath the attic bulb a vast shadow bobbed towards them.

Anne screamed, her dreadful silence broken. "It's Mum!" said Alice. "It's Mum!" Anne sobbed, suddenly limp, and they helped her across the floorboards, then step by step on the beams.

Mother bent to Anne. She looked at Alice, then her gaze found the door shut tight in the wall.

"It's in there," said Alice.

"Put Anne to bed," said Mother. "Blanket switched on."

"Dad –"

"You must stay with Anne, darling."

"But Dad's outside –"

"I will get him," said Mother calmly. "Now do what you're told."

Mother left Alice at the linen cupboard door, and ran.

"Come on, Midget. Everything's all right. Get these clothes off. Apron first."

"I was so scared!"

Alice switched on the electric blanket.

148

"I prayed! And crossed my fingers."

"Off with the jumper."

"Don't leave me!"

"I won't." Alice pushed a log into the fire. She sprinkled on leaves from a supply they had stored in the utility room to dry. The fire flared.

Anne slipped into bed. "I'm cold. Come in beside me."

Alice kicked off her boots and held Anne, warming her.

Then Mother came, and Dad, whispering anxious questions, teapot on the tray, and they sat together on the bed, sugar upon sugar into the mugs – "It's the very thing for shock," said Mother, and the questions stopped when it was clear that Anne was fine, except for the whiteness of her face and the occasional shudder.

She snuggled down. Mother and Dad left. Alice, an arm around her friend, sat up in bed, staring at the fire.

TWENTY-NINE

Alice thought very little. The fire delighted her. The simple wood panelling of the walls and ceiling pleased her eye. The window deep in the wall, with little square panes strong in their frames, was just right. She was untroubled by the thing in the pottery. It would stay there until Melanie was ready.

Her eyes blinked sleepily. She was hungry. She remembered it wasn't even teatime, though night's darkness pressed against the window, and the fire danced. She blinked again, staring, then smiling.

On the table stood shapes that hadn't been there a moment before. Alice recognized Coke cans and a plateful of sandwiches. And she was lying down now, not sitting. Fancy falling asleep then waking, and not knowing!

She slid from bed, tucking the cover against Anne. The electric blanket was switched off. The log lay half eaten by flames. She took a Coke and a sandwich, fizzing the Coke open, spinning the ring-pull into the fire. She walked to the window, and found the shadow of the castle on the snow. A white moon poured down dazzling light, and stars glittered in the purple blackness above the sea. Every stone of the crumbling wall was inked with shadow. Every slope of roof lay softly-white and perfectly drawn by Nature's night-time artist. The padlock shone pretending innocence. Pretending that no ghost lurked behind its shut door.

150

"Alice."

"I'm over here. There's grub on the table."

"What are you doing?"

"Just looking. The castle is beautiful in the moonlight."

"Do you think we'll ever be safe from that thing?"

"Melanie will do something. Are you getting up?"

"I'm cold."

Alice moved through the firelight and passed Anne a sandwich and a drink.

"I wonder what time it is," whispered Anne.

"I don't know. Not late. There's a light in the kitchen."

"Do you think the kiln will be safe?"

"Melanie said it could stay on all night. Though we didn't shut the bungs. Or turn the heat to low."

"So long as our lovely castle doesn't burn down. Good sandwich."

They ate until Alice's fingernails struck china instead of bread.

She crinkled her Coke can.

"Alice."

"Mm."

"Why aren't you afraid?"

Alice looked towards the bed. In the firelight Anne's eyes were huge and dark.

"I was scared at first. Then Melanie said that fear opens a gate. I seemed to know what she meant. Though I don't think I could explain."

"But how do you stop being afraid? I try so hard, but in the pottery I was so scared, I couldn't

151

move. I couldn't speak. Even when you whispered my name. I had to wait till you came near."

"Were you up the stairs when it came in?"

"Just. I was looking for a wire to cut the clay, and the lights. . . As if it was sucking the life from them. I hid, hoping you would come."

"Sorry," said Alice, thinking of the pottery door she had left open.

"But you came! You came right in! I couldn't have done that! How can you stop being afraid?"

The fire continued dancing, as if music played that Alice could not hear.

"I suppose . . ." Alice hadn't thought about it.

She tried to imagine her feelings as she had crept between the shelves into the gloom of the pottery store.

"I wasn't really thinking about . . . about me. I wanted you to be safe."

She looked at Anne, with her eyes so dark, her little face intent, demanding to know, desperate, even, to know how to be unafraid. "I just wasn't thinking about myself," said Alice simply.

"D'you fancy a walk?" Alice, gazing from the window, watched shadows lean as the moon crept across the sky.

"Outside?" cried Anne.

"I want to walk round the castle," said Alice. "Right round." She faced the bed. "It's quite safe."

"It's dark," whispered Anne.

"There's plenty of moonlight. How do you feel?"

"OK."

152

"Afterwards, we'll get something else to eat. A pudding."

"I'm not sure."

"You like pudding."

"About going out."

"I can go myself."

Alice looked from the window, giving her friend time to decide. In the moonlight she saw the padlock hanging by its metal finger.

The bed creaked. Alice turned.

Anne was on the floor at the fire. Flames leapt in celebration. "There's nothing scary about walking," she said.

Alice smiled. They got ready, then went through the house, being fearless, being delighted by their Christmas tree gleaming on the woodwork, sending its light to touch the snow outside.

They closed the door beneath the arch, stepping into moon-glow in the courtyard. "It's so bright!" whispered Anne, and Alice nodded.

She led across the courtyard, avoiding the light from the kitchen window, seeing Mother and Dad drinking coffee.

They crunched over snow, Anne stepping quickly as they neared the coach house, Alice stopping, forcing Anne to wait or walk alone.

She waited, and they stood beneath the moon, breathing whitely.

"I can hear the kiln," whispered Anne.

Alice nodded. She turned her back on the coach house and saw the log pile, like a heap of silver pigs, and the castle's chimneys puffing smoke among the stars.

They left the courtyard by the gap in the wall,
waved to Melanie's cottage, and walked crisp-
footed along the front of the castle where they
looked in on the Christmas tree and the fires
frantic at either end of the long room. The ridge of
snow pushed up by the great door, was hard-
frozen and excellent for balancing on – for a
moment. Then the gloom of the bowing trees made
them move on, round the corner of the castle
where even Alice shivered in the presence of the
orchard by moonlight.

"Rows of witches, right enough!" she breathed,
as Anne stood close.

They walked among the witches' fingers, then
ran joyfully from the orchard to stand on the grass
above the shore, gasping, astonished at the magni-
ficence of the sea at night.

"Isn't this amazing!" whispered Alice. Her arms
embraced everything from the sea to the bowing
trees, from the castle to the glittering black sky. She
ran, Anne following along the snow-thick grass, in
the shadow of the castle wall, seeing the little
turrets, so important looking, but containing
nothing but rubbish. Melanie's cottage again, and
the graveyard, and leaning on the castle wall, the
hothouse.

Anne shied from the hothouse. Dead tomato
plants pressed against the glass, taller than the
girls, trying to get at them. "I don't like that!"
hissed Anne.

They walked beside the hothouse.

Alice shivered as if the graveyard were extra cold
and was drawing heat from her.

They were close to the gap in the wall.

"I could eat a big plate of boiling hot custard," whispered Anne.

Alice didn't reply.

Her skin tingled.

She held Anne's arm, making her stand still. Then she pushed gently, edging her into the shadow of the wall.

All over her body, Alice's flesh was sending out alarms.

She heard Anne draw in a breath to speak.

"Ssh!" she said.

They waited.

THIRTY

The moon stared down.

Alice glanced up, but the stone globe dazzled her, and she frowned, searching the graveyard, and Melanie's garden.

Beneath the trees she stared, fearing to see a loping darkness detach itself and come racing over the snow.

But the trees leaned silently away, prettily silver by moonlight. Tomato plants pressed dead hands against the hothouse glass.

"It can't have escaped!" whispered Anne.

Alice shook her head. Something, she knew, was happening, but it couldn't be that thing – could it? There was no exit from the coach house.

Something moved on the path from Melanie's front door. Alice tugged Anne's sleeve, and they retreated, Alice touching glass and paint-rough timber as she pushed Anne through the part-open door of the hothouse.

They pressed among the horrid plants, and rubbed clean circles on the glass.

"I can't see properly!" whispered Anne. "I hate this! Is it Melanie?"

Alice scowled, not blinking, trying to adjust the movement she saw into a sensible shape. Surely it was Melanie? But the moonlight glanced through it and it couldn't be Melanie; though the limbs swung gracefully, lithe like a young tree . . .

"Of course it's Melanie!" sighed Alice, and Anne

laughed with relief.

But they crouched among dead leaves, watching, and Alice's eye rose for a moment to the bright orb that was the moon, then back to the figure that was Melanie approaching over the snowy mounds of the graveyard. Alice saw her clearly, and wondered why, on such a freezing night, Melanie wandered in her dress and apron. Her spectacles gleamed. Her blonde hair shifted as she walked – she walked past, five paces from the hothouse door, through the gap in the castle wall and out of sight.

"Well!" sighed Alice. "I just don't know! My nerves are giving up! Melanie! I could scoff that pudding!"

They squeezed from the hothouse and stepped through the gap, Alice suddenly hurrying at the thought of Melanie opening the pottery to check the kiln. But Melanie had vanished, and the padlock – its shadow in a different position because the moon had moved – still hung by the metal finger.

The girls went in the kitchen door.

"We thought you were asleep!" cried Mother.

"We ate the sandwiches," said Alice.

"Your father's checking the fires. It's time for bed really – though . . ." Mother's glance went to the window and Alice knew she feared the thing in the coach house.

"The sandwiches were very good," said Anne, and Mother smiled.

"Is there any custard?" asked Alice. "We'll make it ourselves."

"There's a packet of instant," said Mother.

"I know where it is!" cried Anne.

"I'll boil the kettle," said Alice. "Is Melanie with Dad?"

"I haven't seen her," said Mother. She looked at Alice. "I thought she couldn't leave the house? That's why you were looking after the pottery?"

"But we saw her. Just a minute ago. She must have come in here."

"She didn't," said Mother.

"Then where is she?" said Alice. "She can't just have disappeared!"

Mother said, "She did before. If you believe –"

"I suppose," said Alice, looking at Anne for agreement, "that she really was pretty spooky – in the pottery."

Anne nodded, then dipped her face, very busy opening the custard.

Alice looked at Mother. Mother made a tiny smile, raised her eyebrows, sighed. "I don't really understand," she admitted. "Dad, perhaps could explain."

"Melanie said no one could explain."

The kettle gurgled and Alice drowned the custard powder while Anne whisked desperately with a fork.

"We'll need a biscuit to put under this," said Alice.

"Take the syrupy ones," said Mother. "I made plenty of them. They're a bit chewy."

"I'll pour!" said Anne. Alice put a biscuit in both pudding plates. She watched the custard fall in a yellow column. Darkness came between her and the plates, making Anne's little hands less real,

turning the custard into something no more important than a film of itself. She gazed around, seeing
Mother as if in a dream – and the kitchen, with its
cupboards and canary-coloured Aga, seemed to
float in the darkness, bright reality diminishing;
then Melanie's voice called from across the universe, *Alice! Alice!*

Alice tried to blink away the dimness, shake the
voice from her head, but the darkness expanded, a
vast bubble, distorting the kitchen, pressing Alice
out of her body . . .

Melanie's voice, thin as a breath of wind,
hopeless as a soul tortured and forgotten, pleading
to an empty sky. Alice caught the words: *It is too
strong! The silver cord darkens! Oh, my Jack! My
Jack! Surely it is not time! Let me go swiftly to the
second death! Alice! Does my voice not cry in your
darkness! Is your strength the strength of a child
that you fail me in this, the dreadful hour! Abac,
Achides, Elohim, Pentessaron!*

Alice felt that her head was being shaken off.
Her name drifted from far away, but no longer
Melanie's voice.

"Alice!" said Mother.

The kitchen was real again.

Before Alice could speak, feet crunched outside.
The kitchen door burst inwards and Jack, his
round face white, tears on his unshaved cheeks,
horror in every action as he rushed at Alice.
"Melanie!" he wept. "My Melanie! You got to
help! Alice! You're the only one! You got to help
my Melanie! She's dying!"

THIRTY-ONE

"Dying!" gasped Mother. But Jack ignored her. Alice cried out as his great hand caught her arm and almost lifted her off the floor. He dragged her, running to the open door.

Alice glimpsed Anne's startled face, then Mother reaching. But Jack was too strong and too quick, and Alice was staggering, not sure whether to be afraid, half carried over the snow, white breath feathering as Jack gasped words she couldn't understand. Then she struggled when he stopped, his free hand grasping the padlock. "No!" yelled Alice. "Let me go!" She screamed and threw all her weight against his grasp, but he roared, jerked the door, and hurled Alice into the coach house.

The pottery.

Alice fell, and slid on the floor.

She lay trembling.

Beside her the kiln clicked and buzzed, a red haze around the vent in its door. The strip lights still fought the darkness, pale as flesh. The air was warm. The gas fire murmured.

Alice, very carefully, stood up, her hands automatically brushing, so slowly, brushing down her clothes, eyes striving to see beyond the table with its bucket and rows of silly pepper pots; striving to see up the wooden stairs.

Her eye touched on the kiln's thermostat. The needle was at twelve hundred and twenty degrees centigrade.

160

She stepped back towards the pottery door. What was Jack thinking of, throwing her in here! What did he imagine she could do! Die, perhaps? Instead of Melanie! Was he murdering her!!

Something moved.

She battered the door.

"You must help Melanie!" yelled Jack. "I'm only doin' what she said!" Alice heard Anne's voice and Mother, screaming.

"Daddy!" howled Alice. "Daddy!"

She looked behind her. Beyond the table, something reared. Two tiny dots of light stared at Alice. The thing had grown. In its blackness she saw faint patterns of paw prints on sand, but it was unreal, and certainly not a leopard; an idea of a leopard, as someone once said, but vague, spreading darkness across the floor. Alice realized that the ghastly thing filled the room.

But the dark centre – which was the coat – reared onto the table, and leapt. Alice could do nothing. It descended on her, over her, around her. She heard Father's voice. She remembered to be fearless.

Fearless.

She opened her eyes and rose swiftly. Fearless, and cold. Her mind as cold as water in the ocean. No surprise at seeing a human body slumped against the door; a young body, eyes shut, soft lashes, ripe figure; her own body; Alice Mason. And in the gloom, shimmering, a silver cord, rising from the Alice Mason on the floor to the Alice Mason in the pottery.

161

The kiln clicked and buzzed. Twelve hundred and twenty-two, said the thermostat's needle.

She heard her name and found Melanie, like a shadow of Melanie, standing, a silver cord lacing out to infinity, but dull, beating with feeble energy.

Help me! I came too soon! I am not ready!

Alice embraced her, finding her solid, finding her cold.

Alice felt love for her friend, and saw Melanie's cord throb with light. The two wandering lines of life pounded in rhythm, but the shadows came crushing around them, darkening the room until Alice could see nothing but the dim rods that were the strip lights and the red haze over the kiln. Then those shrank as the darkness sucked, and the silver cords shrivelled.

Melanie's voice drifted in a distant cry of gratitude and despair.

We are not strong enough! But there is still time for you! Go back! Go back!

Alice remembered the fury that had vanquished the coat when Mother came with the car. She remembered the energy erupting from the roots of her existence. And she screamed, streaming that energy outward.

The cords pulsed gloriously, pushing back the darkness, letting the strip lights and the kiln shine suddenly, and a roar, which Alice knew no earthly ear could hear, struck her astral body setting her flesh vibrating, killing the scream in her throat, draining her, darkening the silver cords.

Melanie's voice cried in the depths of the galaxy, words Alice could not hear, but Alice was gone in an instant from the pottery, and before her glittered the sea.

Her mind was too cold to be startled. One moment she was holding Melanie, the next, she was in the graveyard.

The castle rose dark behind the dull shine of the hothouse.

Melanie has put me here. But why?

Then Alice remembered oh! a long time ago! Melanie saying that in the graveyard, energy waited to be used. At the thought, Alice writhed as power flowed up into her, and the ground stirred, it seemed, with the shifting of the restless dead.

But Melanie was dead.

Her cord was black.

Too late! Darkness is the end! Striving is useless! We all die –

Alice's mouth twisted into a snarl.

These are not my thoughts! I defy you! Darkness cannot overcome light! I am light! MELANIE!

The sea vanished.

The kiln clicked. Its eye was dark. The strip lights were dull glass.

The thinnest of pale lines led Alice to Melanie. She embraced Melanie and the energy of the graveyard's ancient battle pulsed through the silver cords, and the darkness moaned.

The moan soared to a scream. Alice thought her astral body would dissolve in the sound, but it was a scream of rage which snapped off, filling the air with quivering silence.

Alice fell into the silence as if she were dropping

into a well, deep inside herself.

As her mind faded, she despaired at seeing movement – like the shadow of an animal – retreating from the rising glow of the strip lights. Her last sight was of the staircase from the store room, and Anne stepping down into the pottery.

Something broke.

The crash opened her eyes.

For one second she saw what was in front of her. The kiln, its gauge suddenly reading fifty degrees, drained of its power; and Anne's little elbows frantic as she prodded into the open kiln with the stick that Melanie used for stirring glaze – *as she stuffed the coat inside!*

Then the coach house door against Alice's back retreated, and she fell outwards, and was instantly gathered into Father's arms.

"Alice! Alice!"

"Darling, are you all right!" from Mother.

Alice sighed.

"She's alive!" said Father. He held her close and lifted her, then ran, and the moon joggled among the chimneys.

They put her to bed.

"Her colour's coming back!" said Mother.

"Pulse is steady," declared Father, and his lean face stared down. "Alice. Can you hear me?"

She blinked slowly. She had stepped out of this world and returned. She gazed up at Daddy. His cheek was swollen.

"Can you hear me?" he said. Anne's face came suddenly close and her arms crushed Alice.

164

Something Watching

Alice remembered Melanie and tried to sit up.
"Melanie!" she gasped. "Is Melanie safe?"
"Are *you* all right!" cried Father.
"Yes! Melanie!"
"I'll find out," said Anne.
Alice lay still. She waited.
She sighed.

THIRTY-TWO

Laughter in the long room.

Laughter around the dining table.

The fireplaces gobbled logs and coal.

The Christmas tree in its thick green dress flickered colours into the night.

"It only 'urts when I larf," said Father, easing his bruised jaw, and stuffing in turkey and cranberry sauce while his mouth was open.

"You know," he continued, "I couldn't believe it when Anne rushed through yelling that you'd thrown Alice into the pottery. I thought you'd gone mad – or she had."

"Sorry about your jaw," said Jack, "but I didn't have no choice. Couldn't have you going after her too soon."

"It was a terrible chance," said Mother doubtfully.

"Oh, Mum!" cried Alice. "You know there was nothing else Jack could do!" She turned to him. "I thought you were trying to murder me! Was I really in there only a few minutes?"

"Long enough," said Father, "for Jack to slug me and rush away with the key in his pocket. It's amazing how difficult it is even in a castle to find something strong enough to break a padlock."

Father looked at Melanie. He stared at her so long that Anne's fingers squeezed Alice's knee beneath the table, and they glanced at each other and giggled into their turkey.

166

"I think Melanie is quite recovered, Dick," said Mother, and Dick turned almost as red as his cranberry sauce. "You are looking very beautiful," said Mother.

"Thank you," said Father.

"Melanie!" yelled Alice, as laughter rose again around the long room.

"And long enough, Alice," announced Father, "– you were long enough in the pottery, I mean – for Anne to find her way through the attics without anyone knowing, and get into the store room. I must admit," said Father, resting his fork, "I was so concerned that I didn't notice what Anne was doing. It only dawned on me when I opened the door to drag you out and there she was slamming the kiln door. Talk about kids!" He stared at Anne, then Alice.

On the table among Grandma's Royal Doulton plates, candles burned, and the wax dribbled suddenly, then froze on the candlesticks.

Father sighed and smiled.

"Could we forget it?" said Mother. "It's Christmas. I would like to enjoy it."

"Anyone ready for more wine? You children are drunk enough." But Father filled everyone's glass. "I was thinking. Melanie – you make pottery for the tourists. What if I were to open part of the castle as a coffee shop . . .?"

"Richard!" said Alice in her best policeman's voice. Anne giggled.

"What's funny about that?"

Laughter in the long room.

The Christmas lights blinked out their message

of hope through the falling snow. The bowing trees sighed. Beyond the graveyard the sea slept, grey and silent. And from the clustered chimneys of the castle, smoke trailed tall through the winter sky.